THE NAVY SEAL BROTHERHOOD

A SEAL Romance

JAMILA JASPER

Illustrated by
DENIA DESIGN

READ BOOK #1 FREE SAMPLE

Visit deniadesign.com for more information about the cover design and cover design services.

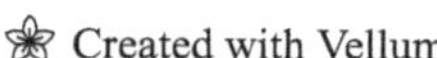
Created with Vellum

Series

The London Brotherhood I

The London Brotherhood II

The London Brotherhood III

The Navy SEAL Brotherhood IV

The Moscow Brotherhood V

Part I

MACE HARWOOD JR.

"I don't want to hear another word of complaint. Usmanov is paying us *each* five figures for a two day trip and I know all of you motherfuckers need the money."

We stood shoulder to shoulder, at attention, as Tyrese walked back and forth in front of us with a mean look in his eye, desperate to convince us that this mission was worth an iota of our time.

"CHUBB!" Tyrese barked, "With the gut you've been putting on, I know you need money for more food."

Chester Chubb turned scarlet. Tyrese stopped in front of Robbie next.

"PEÑA! Your mamá needs her rent paid and we all know it. If you stopped spending money on liquor and girls, maybe you wouldn't still be here."

Robbie didn't flinch at Tyrese's denigrations. By now we

were all accustomed to his method of motivation. Tyrese's boots crunched into the earth.

"HARWOOD! You don't need the money, but you're a crazy motherfucker and we can't do this shit without you."

"YES, SIR!" I replied.

Tyrese continued.

"ELLIS! We need you 'cause you've got a kid in every country your sorry ass set foot in, and when these ladies come knocking on your door for child support, you'll need every dime you can get."

"YES, SIR!" Bubba Ellis shouted, with a vigor that only a man who has successfully dodged child support in multiple countries for a decade could muster.

"ZHANG! Stand up straighter, boy. We need you more than anybody 'cause you're the only motherfucker who can keep these bastards in line. NOW, DOES ANYONE HAVE ANY MORE COMPLAINTS?"

"NO, SIR!" We responded in unison.

"Excellent. At ease, gentlemen. Let's review the mission after training tomorrow. I want all of you there at 0800 sharp."

"YES, SIR."

"Good. You're dismissed."

An intense morning workout left all of us dripping in sweat. Six months ago, we'd begun our work as a team rooting out Arabs in the desert and tracking Syrian ex-pats who might have been spies out in Kuwait. Our last teams had… disintegrated so to speak. Tyrese and I were the only ones to survive a mishap out in Iraq, and he'd been promoted to team leader of this new band of America's most dangerous soldiers. SEAL Team Gamma formed six months ago and since then we'd been on mission after mission in the desert, interspersed with week-long training camps in the harshest climates in the world, from the Australian outback to Siberia. When we heard about Tyrese's latest plan for us while we waited for our next government contract, none of us were thrilled.

In the locker room after our intense workout, we stripped down, except Ellis, who never showered after workouts, and lathered up. Peña was pissed. So was Chubb. Zhang never let anything ruffle him and didn't talk much anyway.

"Lorde has lost his damn mind," Chubb grunted with his harsh Georgia twang.

"A princess," Peña sneered, "We're America's most dangerous soldiers, and he expects us to transport a fucking princess."

"He's lost his damn mind," Chubb replied.

Zhang added calmly, "We're getting paid, at least. Well."

"Fuckin' chinks only care about money," Chubb sneered.

"Watch your language," I retorted, "That 'chink' is your brother."

"Whatever," Chubb replied, "Ain't like he minds."

Tim Zhang remained quiet, coating his body in soap. We'd lost our shyness about showering together during bootcamp. It made no difference who was naked and for how long anymore. We'd seen too much together and been in too many situations where showers were never an option to be too particular about it.

"We leave tomorrow too. A Russian princess, what the hell does she look like you think?" Chubb asked.

Peña snickered, "I'm sure you'd like to give it to her but you've got to get through Ellis first."

Chubb hollered, "Ellis? That motherfucker can't have any more kids without his wife losing her damn mind on him. I know women, Penny, I know women."

"What do you know about women, Chubb?"

"Hey, I'm married, motherfucker. I've been married. More than you can say."

"I don't need marriage to get what I want from women."

"OHHH!"

"Shut up, Penny," Chubb snarled.

He'd never learned to pronounce Robbie's last name right so he called him whatever his little Southern mind told him too — often some butchered version of Robbie's actual name. This week he'd settled on "Penny".

"She's a spoiled Russian princess," I reminded them, "It'll be over and done with in two days. It can't be that bad."

"I'm sure she looks like Ivanka," Chubb said.

Robbie and I wrinkled our noses in disgust.

"Ivanka Trump looks like the bottom of my shoe," Robbie snickered.

I couldn't help but crack a smile, knowing that it wouldn't take more than that to get under Chubb's skin. He threw a punch, and Robbie dodged it easily. Robbie tossed the soap to me and I lathered up, cracking a smile as I watched the two idiots try to wrestle each other naked. Robbie at least, seemed to be enjoying himself. Chubb finally caught hold of him and threatened him, but before he could land an actual punch, Robbie managed to diffuse the guy's anger and he let go.

"Fuckin' beaner," Chubb muttered under his breath.

"Careful," Robbie replied.

Chubb scowled, but he didn't push Robbie any further. We left the locker and went our separate ways. I didn't say much, but I had my own questions about what Tyrese was playing at. He didn't explain it too well when I asked him privately. All I heard was that he owed someone — not the Russian — and that this man, some Oliver Cook, had saved his ass a long time ago. He owed him, and now, we were about to fly some Russian chick from New York City to Europe. This wasn't exactly in the purview of the SEALs usually, except this woman's father was a Russian oligarch and a US diplomat, with enough clout in the country to make it a matter of national security. It didn't make much sense to me, but it wasn't my place to question my team leader.

We had all we needed to know: One Russian chick needed to be brought safely from point A to point B. We had permission from Tyrese and high command to do the job, and once we were done, we'd get paid enough money to kick back and relax.

The next morning, I woke up at 0400, did calisthenics until I couldn't breathe and then I pumped iron until my muscles shook. An easy mission like this meant busting my balls in the gym so I didn't get lazy. I finished my workout a 0630 and downed breakfast: a protein shake with raw eggs, spinach, goat milk and ice. A day hasn't begun until I've worked myself to the bone. The addiction to the endorphins kept my ass out of all the trouble liquor tried to get me into.

I showed up at the meeting place at 0745. Zhang was the only one there. He crouched outside the building in a squat with his eyes closed.

"What are you doing, fuckin' meditating?"

Zhang opened one eye.

"Good morning, Mace."

"Where are the guys?"

"Not here."

"Not even Tyrese?"

"No."

"Mind getting on your feet?"

Zhang rose slowly out of his squat, balancing on one foot before putting the other down.

"You're a fuckin' freak show, Zhang."

"Thank you."

"Wasn't a compliment."

"I know," Zhang replied.

Man that guy didn't let anyone ruffle his feathers. Not even me. We waited a few more minutes. Robbie showed up next, then Tyrese, then Chubb, then Ellis. Our six man team assembled right at 0758 — early enough not to cause Tyrese to blow a fuse.

"Now that you're all here, we'll go to the office across the street. Look smart fellas. Usmanov is a tough guy and despite his protected status by our government, don't think for an instant that he isn't dangerous. Any perceived slight and I can't control what happens to you. Do you understand?"

"Yes, sir!" Our voices sounded in perfect unison, like our training had taught us. We were one voice and one brotherhood whenever we wore the uniform. We walked in single file, steps in line with one another across the street. This part of the city was barely awake. An old Jewish woman selling roses was the only sign of life. She pretended not to be eyeing us curiously, but I could sense we were an unusual sight for this part of the city. Tyrese rapped his fists against an old wooden door.

A voice barked back in Russian. Tyrese responded some mumbo-jumbo I couldn't understand and then the door opened. A dark haired man with icy blue eyes glowered at us and spat a single English word.

"Identification."

"Fellas, pull 'em out," Tyrese commanded.

We pulled out our IDs and the Russian checked them like he meant it. One at a time, he allowed us in. They were all armed, though if we'd meant business, their weapons wouldn't have done any good. Each of us could take down three grown men, weapons or not. We were warriors. Guns were just a bonus. We walked down a long hallway. The deeper we got into the house (if you could call it that) the stronger the stench of vodka. At the end of the hallway, the fella who led us there pushed the door open and we entered a large study. Tyrese whistled and the six of us stood shoulder to shoulder in order of rank.

It was clear who the Russian was, but I couldn't figure out where his daughter was. He had a young woman standing next to him. I assumed she was his mistress. Her skin was dark, so dark that it was almost purple. She was tall, too. And skinny.

"Mister Usmanov, thank you for agreeing to meet with us. These men are the proud soldiers of SEAL Team Gamma. They're brave, smart, and best suited for the protection of your daughter."

Oleg nodded.

"*Spasibo.*"

His soldier left the room. We stood at attention, looking Oleg Usmanov dead in the eye.

"Introduce yourselves," he commanded, taking the reins of leadership from Tyrese effortlessly.

"Robert Pena, sir."

"Thomas Zhang, sir."

"Mace Harwood, sir."

"Chester Chubb, sir."

"Bubba Ellis, sir."

Oleg nodded.

"Milena, step forward."

The dark-skinned woman standing next to him took a step forward.

"This is my daughter, Milena Aminata Usmanov."

The dark-skinned girl bowed her head.

"Hello," she said quietly.

None of us dared say a word, but we were all thinking it. How the hell could a man the color of a fresh snow have a daughter as dark as a blackberry. Tyrese held his head high, as Oleg stared at each one of us, analyzing us with a vicious stare. I could smell the vodka on his breath, but he was by no means drunk. He walked down the line of us, just like Tyrese did.

"I want you to take my daughter away tonight. Do you understand?"

We paused for a beat. Tyrese nodded.

"Yes, sir!"

"If anything happens to her, I have your names. I know your families. Even you, Mister Ellis, I know how many children you have. I can name more of your children than you can. Da?"

"Yes, sir!" We repeated.

"Take care of my daughter. If not, I do not need to say what will happen. Da?"

"Yes, sir!"

"Good."

Oleg rested his hand on his daughter's shoulder.

"Aminata, you are to go with these men."

"Papa!?"

"Aminata, we discussed this. You are in danger. I promised protection."

"I expected bodyguards, not this."

She still hadn't looked us in the eye. Oleg rested a hand on his daughter's shoulder and she brusquely brushed him off.

"No. I will not go with them."

"This is not discussion, Aminata," he growled, his English slipping as his daughter's disobedience turned his cheeks a flush mauve.

"I don't see why I have to leave."

"It is not safe," Oleg growled, visibly unamused to have his word questioned in front of his fresh hires.

"I am *not* going to leave, papa. You can't make me!"

Her accent was surprisingly cosmopolitan. Except when she said papa, she would have sounded completely American, but with a nondescript accent that only comes from picking up the sounds of intonations of Americans from Texas to Boston.

Oleg removed his hand from his daughter's shoulders forlornly.

"I'm sorry, Milena."

Her expression softened.

"Papa—"

Oleg interrupted her before she could continue.

"Gentlemen, are you ready to prove you're worth the money I spent?"

We waited for his command.

"Take her."

"Sir, take her?"

"By any means necessary — without harming her," he added the last bit as an afterthought.

Hearing her papa suggest that she was now at our mercy sent the poor woman into what can only be described as a fit of madness. Her eyes widened and she turned away from us, forgetting the dignity and manners that had made her seem so poised and collected before. She screamed at her father.

"Papa, are you crazy!"

"I'm sorry, Aminata."

"You're crazy! None of you will tell me what's going on. Not Vasily! Not Feodor!"

Tyrese nodded and Bubba Ellis lunged forward and grabbed the woman around her waist.

"PUT. ME. DOWN."

Oleg nodded and muttered, "Gentlemen…" before exiting the room. I guess he wanted us to do the dirty work but that didn't mean he had to sit there and watch it happen before his very eyes. His daughter's squealing hadn't let up. Despite his size, Bubba struggled to hold onto her.

Robbie jumped in to help Ellis, and kicking and screaming, we took her out of the building and tossed her in the back of the car. The old Jewish woman was no longer selling her flowers, and the streets were empty. In the back of the sound-proof vehicle, Robbie and Bubba sat on either side of her. I hopped into the driver's seat and Tyrese in the passenger side. The other two followed in their own car. We put up the partition between the two of us, drowning out her sound even further.

Despite all that, she screamed for a full hour before she must have tired out and fallen asleep. Ellis put the partition down just a tad after she was quiet. Yes, she was definitely asleep.

"Got ourselves a screamer, haven't we," he joked with a crude snicker.

Tyrese glared at him in the rearview mirror, "I expect better from you, Ellis."

"Yes, sir."

"Keep in mind that Oleg Usmanov is perfectly capable of ending you. If he doesn't do it by the blade, he'll make sure every bitch you knocked up from Chattanooga to Sydney is knocking at your door for child support."

That shut Bubba right up.

We took her to Tyrese's spot. He normally rents a place the night before big trips. We spend the night together, all of us, reviewing our plans before shipping out. Tonight, we didn't expect to have to do much. I mean, the plan was simple. We'd fly out to Bermuda, drive to the estate that Oleg had cleared out for us, then we'd go by boat for a day until we got to the private island where we'd have armed guards and a pretty little cage for our dove.

When the car pulled into the private garage at Tyrese's hideout spot for us, Aminata woke up in the back seat. She was forlorn, like she'd given up completely on any chance of escape. No more kicking, cussing, screaming or biting. She didn't say a word. Robbie spoke to her gently.

"Ma'am, we've got to take you inside now."

He opened the door and she stepped out of her own accord. Robbie and Bubba didn't know what to make of it, so they kept their distance. Tyrese opened the side door and led her into the tiny house.

"The bedrooms are upstairs. Ellis, Peña, you're on kitchen duty. Chubb, Zhang, I'll need you two with me. Harwood, you take the lady upstairs and stand guard."

"But, sir—"

"Don't question me, Harwood, I don't have time," Tyrese snapped back.

"Yes, sir."

The men split off and Aminata turned to look at me with revulsion and contempt.

"Miss Usmanov, come with me."

She glowered, but followed, walking at my side as I wove through the house searching for the stairs. I took her upstairs to her bedroom. It was easy to spot which one Tyrese intended for her. Tactically, it was the one where she was most likely to be safe. Only one small window, high off the ground, isolated from the other rooms but close to the stairs if she needed to get out of dodge quick.

"These are your quarters ma'am. Make yourself comfortable and if you need a little privacy, I'll turn around."

"Turn around?" She snapped.

"I apologize, ma'am, but it's my responsibility to keep an eye on you at all times."

"What if I need to use the restroom?" She replied in a haughty, indignant tone.

"Well, ma'am, you'll have to do it with my back turned."

She looked mortified.

"Don't worry ma'am, this only applies on U.S. Soil. We'll be out of the danger zone soon.

"Comforting," Aminata sniffed.

"Ma'am, I'm Mace Harwood and I'm at your service for the night. I know this may come as a shock to you, but my men and I are the best of the best and we'll assure no harm comes to you."

"No harm? What are you talking about? Why is everyone acting like I'm in danger?"

Her confusion and fear seemed genuine. Even if it didn't make much sense to me. Her father was a dangerous man. Tyrese had pulled up his file and despite his diplomatic immunity, Uncle Sam had information on this guy that could make a soldier's blood curdle. He was cold. Ruthless. Possibly the most dangerous man in all of Russia, aside from Putin himself. This woman couldn't have made it to thirty-something years old without knowing the truth about him.

"I'm sure you know about your father's business dealings," I replied, diplomatically, testing out the waters of what Miss Usmanov knew, or what she was prepared to admit to herself. I could smell onions sautéing downstairs and hear Chubb and Peña arguing over how long to cook pasta. I pushed the door closed, leaving it ajar slightly.

"My father is a diplomat," she responded in genuine confusion, "His business dealings are all perfectly legal."

I couldn't help but smirk. She was just so convinced. I'd seen pictures of the tongues her father had cut out on his own. He cozied up with the biggest mob bosses in Russia and he'd been this way for decades.

"Right," I replied, "Well in that case, your angelic father has gotten himself in hot water and he no longer believes that you're safe."

"Is this because of what happened in London?"

"What happened in London?"

"I was with my brother, Feodor. We were *robbed*. Papa became so paranoid after that."

"Robbed, you say?"

"Da. English lads. And a woman… or two women… They let me go."

"They killed your brother?"

"No. But he was hurt."

"Hm."

"You don't believe me?"

"I believe you, ma'am. Maybe there's more to the story."

"Papa explained it all to me. We were targeted because of our wealth."

"Whatever you say, ma'am."

"Stop calling me ma'am," she snapped.

"What do you want me to call you then? Milena? Aminata? Miss Usmanov?"

"Not Milena. That is for family, only. Aminata is fine, or Amy. I go by Amy when I'm in America."

"Amy. That's sweet."

"I'm not trying to be sweet."

She folded her arms and huffed, heading over to the small window and peering out.

"Papa always has to be so extreme."

"Right. Well it's obvious he loves you."

"He always has," she replied fiercely, "My biological father worked for Papa, and when he died, Papa took me in without a doubt."

"What sort of work did your father do for Oleg?"

"I don't know."

I did. All of it was written in her file. Aminata was genuinely ignorant to all of it. I wondered how her father had managed to keep her ignorant.

"Don't you worry about it then. I'm sure he has good reasons for wanting to protect you."

"It's cruel. I am ripped from everything I love. My brothers won't answer my questions. It's infuriating."

She wrinkled her nose and I couldn't help but feel something stir in me as she shook her head in frustration and her hair brushed over her shoulders, cascading down her back in thick, tight curls. She turned to face me and for the first time, I noticed her unusual eyes. Her skin was a dark shade of brown, but her eyes were grey.

"Wow," I muttered.

The word escaped from my lips.

"What?"

It was too late now. I had to tell her or risk her thinking I was some kind of nut.

"Your eyes. They're…"

"Grey?"

"Yeah."

"Papa explained it's a rare mutation in my mother's tribe in Sudan. One in every six children is born with grey eyes."

"Sudan?"

"Well you didn't think my biological father was Russian, did you?"

"Not at all."

"My mother was from South Sudan. She died a few months after I was born. During the civil war."

"Sorry."

"You're staring," she snapped.

"I can't help it," I replied honestly.

"It's unnerving."

"I've never seen eyes like that on—"

"A girl this dark?"

"Sorry to be rude, ma— Amy."

"I'm used to it. Do you know what I've been through being this dark in Russia?"

"I can't imagine," I replied.

"You're right," she sniffed, "You can't."

"Your skin is beautiful," I offered, unsure of what to say.

She rolled her eyes, "Oh what a consolation prize. A white man finds my skin beautiful. Everything is all better now."

"That's not what I meant."

"I know what you meant. And maybe it's not such a good idea for you to flirt with the person you're obligated to protect."

Damn, she was a spitfire. The more she tried to get me to back off, the more I wanted to chase her. It's simple biology. Men are hard-wired to chase and a woman like Aminata doesn't stumble onto your path very often. The SEALs are kind of a sausage fest if you get my drift. Now guys like Robbie mightn't mind that, but I did.

"Sorry if I offended you, Amy."

I kept my eyes on her, staring into those steel grey eyes. If she hadn't been my ward, I would have reached out to touch her face, just to see if it was really as soft as it looked.

"Careful, Harwood. You don't want to land in any trouble."

"The name's Mace. And trouble don't scare me one bit."

I winked at her and she looked away from me bashfully and went back to staring out her small window, fidgeting with her bracelet as she dreamed wistfully of escape, or perhaps began to question her father's stories and come closer to understanding the truth.

Tyrese relieved me of my duties around dinner time. He brought supper for Aminata, and I went downstairs to enjoy a feast with the boys. They all had their own opinions about her, and I couldn't blame them even if I didn't agree. They saw a spoiled, confused, rich girl without enough sense to realize the truth about her father. I saw someone else.

She was sheltered, sure. Naive? Definitely. But there was something strong behind those eyes that spoke to her desire to be free. I didn't join in their ragging on her, and when Tyrese poked his head in, we all shut up.

"I expect all of you up at 0400 hours. Mace, she seems to have taken a liking to you, so you're responsible for getting her on the plane. She has no idea where we're going, and I want you to expect resistance. Do whatever you must without harming her."

"Yes, sir."

Tyrese continued, "And I want you all in uniform tomorrow. This might be a private endeavor but it is work and you are still representing the U.S. Navy. Do you understand?"

"Yes, sir."

"You're dismissed for the night. But no hootin' and hollerin' 'til late."

"Yes, sir."

Tyrese returned upstairs. Chubb, Zhang and Ellis wanted to drink, but I couldn't think about anything but sleep. Robbie and I retired to our cots. I fell asleep to the sound of Robbie praying in Spanish under his breath.

I woke up without an alarm at 0330. After a decade of life in the Navy, I didn't need an alarm to get my ass out of bed. The other guys would be up after me. I did a quick 200 pushups and washed my face before I went upstairs to wake Amy. She opened the door, her grey eyes puffy , red and swollen.

"What do you want?"

"It's time to get out of here."

"Where are we going?"

"We're moving you. We're leaving the country today and we've got wheels up at 0445."

"A flight?"

"Come on, get dressed. We don't have a lot of time."

Aminata snapped, "I'm not going to get dressed until you tell me where we're going."

"We're going to Bermuda."

"Bermuda?!"

"It's not our final destination."

"Where is?"

"I can't disclose that. Not while you're a flight risk."

"Then I'm not leaving," Amy replied.

"What could I do to convince you?"

"Nothing."

"Nothing?" I asked, "What if I promised to tell you about your father."

"What about my father?"

"I will tell you the truth about who your father is."

"My father is Oleg Usmanov, a diplomat and a successful Russian businessman."

"But something in your heart tells you that's not the entire story, right?"

"N-no."

"Don't lie."

"If I come with you, you'll tell me everything?"

"Everything I know."

"Fine. I'll come with you."

"Atta girl."

Aminata glowered. She shut the door and then emerged a few

minutes later, dressed.

"I'll need to take a shower, at some point."

"You can do that when we land."

That seemed to satisfy her. Tyrese seemed impressed when I got her into the car on time so we could drive to the private airstrip. The other fellas were too tired to be impressed. Zhang, Ellis and Chubb had been up all night drinking, and hadn't had a lick of sleep. Robbie was never worth shit in the mornings. Tyrese was intently focused on our goal for the day and not much for conversation. Aminata sat in the backseat between Robbie and Bubba Ellis again.

We arrived at the airport and once we filed out of the car, dressed in uniform with fresh buzzcuts and aftershave on our faces, Aminata stuck by my side.

"I don't know how long this flight is, but I'm sitting next to you."

"Sure about that?"

"No. But I know you made me promise and if you want me to ever trust you again, you're going to have to keep it."

"Got it."

She had a little attitude that I knew the other fellas didn't like, but she was a spitfire and Harwood men tend to be partial to them. The small private plane waited at the end of the landing strip.

"That's my father's plane," Aminata muttered.

"Yes, he's sent it for you."

"Is Hal flying it?"

"No. Ellis is."

"That guy?" She replied, wrinkling her nose in disgust.

"Trust me, he's a better pilot than he looks."

"I have no choice but you trust you?"

"Get on that plane, Amy, and I'll give you the answers you need."

I got her on the plane and she sat next to me. Ellis stepped in as pilot with Tyrese sitting next to him. Robbie sat in front of us and he turned around to face Aminata.

"Good morning, Miss Usmanov. Ready for our flight today?" Robbie asked.

"Yes. Thank you for asking," Aminata said softly.

"Slept well?"

"Yes."

"Quiet one, aren't ya?"

Aminata didn't respond and Robbie tucked in, ready to go back to sleep. Within twenty minutes we were in the air. Take off was shaky. I found myself wishing that Bubba had more sleep.

She said, "So. You made me a promise. I want you to deliver."

"Right. Your father."

"What do you mean, I don't know who he really is?"

"Your father's a diplomat, Amy. That much is true. But he's also the leader of the largest mafia family in Russia."

Amy snorted and then full-on laughed.

"Really? You think I'm that stupid? Nice job using that to get me on the plane."

"I'm not joking."

"My father? The mafia? My father wouldn't hurt a fly. He's *vegan.*"

"Vegan or not, he's an Usmanov."

"Exactly. Oleg Usmanov. He's gentle. He rescued me from certain death when I was a child. I would have been an orphan if it weren't for him."

"Have you ever asked yourself why your father rescued you? The real reason?"

"He knew my biological father well. They were friends."

"Your biological father was a mercenary."

"You're lying."

"I'm not lying, Aminata."

"I'm not going to listen to this. I'm not going to listen to lies about my father."

"Then don't listen. It ain't gonna affect me."

MILENA AMINATA USMANOV

My skin is dark. The children at school would all gather around and touch me, mesmerized by the color. I would curl up, retreating into myself as they grew enchanted by the unfamiliar, or on occasion, disgusted. I was alone often.

My father, Oleg, did everything in his power to make sure that as soon as I was old enough, I would go somewhere else where I could fit in. First it was boarding school in Switzerland. As he left me with the nuns, I grabbed onto his coattails and screamed, wailing throughout the dormitory when I overheard another student, a pale blonde haired girl with a pink upturned nose whisper to another, "Sie schreit, aber sie errötet nicht einmal."

She's screaming, but she doesn't even blush, they said. Again, I was marked as an outsider, with my thick Moscow accent, the way my tongue stumbled over French and English as I wrestled my way through confusing articles and unfamiliar syllables thrust together in an unnatural way.

In Switzerland, I learned the reason for my fellow students discomfort.

"If you're Russian, why are you black?"

I looked back at her puzzled. I'd known my skin was different from everyone else's, but there had never been anyone black in Russia to explain to me what that meant. All I knew was that I was different and the people like me were far away on some strange continent called Africa where my father once had business. He told me that my mother was from South Sudan, and I nodded, even if I had no idea where South Sudan was, and what kind of people were there. I was raised Russian, through and through.

Papa gave me vodka when I had a cold, and vodka when I had my first heartbreak. I grew up eating pelmeni and snowshoeing during the winters, and vacationing with Papa to

Ukraine, or to a villa on the Southern coast of Croatia. I enjoy borscht as much as my brothers and I can shoot just like they can — although I never took to duck hunting the way Papa hoped.

Despite what everyone told me about the color of my skin, Papa never made me believe for a moment that I wasn't Russian, through and through.

After a painful four years at boarding school in Switzerland where I longed for the view of St Basil's near Papa's city apartment, or the views in front of the Kremlin as we drove past to go to visit babushka at her penthouse, Papa made new plans for my education. In Switzerland, I'd heard all about America from some of the other girls. Papa preferred European and Asian travel, so while I'd been everywhere from Tokyo to Montenegro, America was still inconceivable to me. The fiction of the rare television programs I saw in Switzerland where the rare exposure I had to American culture until Papa sent me over there for boarding school.

At the time, I never questioned why Papa had only sent me, and never Vasily, or Feodor, or Boris. Papa kept my brothers at his side and I never thought him to be hiding anything. I never saw him enough to think he was. Strange things did happen during my childhood, but Papa always managed to quiet my doubts.

I thought the events of my life through all over again, up until when I left for America. That weekend, Feodor had been hurt badly, and Papa told me there had been an attempt on his life due to his new position as a diplomat. At boarding school, I rarely went back to Russia. Papa placated my homesickness with trips to New York, Miami, and San Francisco.

For the first time in my life, I saw women and girls who looked like me. I learned how to wear my hair long for the first time. But to these women, I was still an oddity. My skin might have been black but I had yet to learn how to shed the Russian accent, and culturally, I had the brutish roughness of a girl who grows up with many brothers and my Russian mannerisms made fitting in with the other dark girls difficult.

I did what I had to and after boarding school, I attended Georgetown where I studied English and perfected my speaking, eliminating all the Russian afflictions from my speech. After that, I worked for a year or two, but then Boris fell sick and I had no choice but to give up the small American life I had built and return to Russia.

Papa seemed anxious that I was there. He offered me money, a free condominium, a car, and even a horse for some odd reason, to return to America. Mace said my father was dangerous and perhaps I had been blind to it. His desire to keep me from Russia was strong, and given Mace's accusations, I settled into the notion that perhaps he had been telling the truth and perhaps my father was not the man that I thought he was.

He was a man who could have been protecting his daughter, but he could have just as easily been protecting me from himself. But then my brothers? Could they really lie to me like this? Feodor could, surely. But not Vasily. Not Boris. I couldn't bring myself to believe that.

I tapped Mace on the shoulder.

"Hm?"

"I want to know more."

"Why? So I can get crucified again?"

The soldier they called Robbie, or sometimes Penny, turned back to look through the seats, his tiny anthracite eyes gleaming with mischief.

"I heard what you told her, Harwood. She won't believe it. She's too naive."

Chester Chubb chuckled.

"Can you believe it? Thinking Oleg Usmanov wouldn't hurt a fly."

The two snickered.

"Quiet, both of you," Mace growled, stepping to my defense.

He touched his hand to my arm gently. "We'll talk about this when we land."

The second his palm touched my arm, strange surges of energy pulsed through me. He closed his eyes and tipped his hat over his head. I swallowed the lump in my throat and didn't bother to sleep. I wouldn't have been able to manage it anyway. As Bermuda came into view from the plane window, I remained the only one awake, as well as the Asian, Tim Zhang, and he didn't bother speaking to me. He stared quietly out at the view just like I did.

With the plane's descent I managed to push all thoughts of my father out of my mind for the time being. These men were taking me against my will for my protection and despite my father's trust in them, I had to be on my toes. If what they hinted at was true, and my father was a dangerous man with dangerous enemies, I wouldn't be safe here or anywhere.

We landed on a private strip and a U.S. Diplomat came to greet us with two tall guards flanking him. As I listened to Tyrese talk with the gentleman, I realized he was former Navy and that connection was what got us on the island virtually unnoticed. We piled into four black jeeps with heavily tinted windows. Chubb was supposed to be driving mine, but Mace made him switch and the rest of them scattered amongst the remaining jeeps to confuse anyone potentially targeting us.

I wondered how much danger I was really in, and how much of this was simply Papa taking extra precautions due to recent hot water. The strange incident with Feodor brought enough questions to the surface, all of which Papa smoothed over. His answers must have been lies, if I were to believe Mace. Given the level of red tape we'd circumvented, I was apt to believe him.

"You good?" Mace asked once we got into the jeep.

I whispered a weak, affirmative response. Of course, nothing was right about this. Of course, the last thing I wanted was to be whisked away from the world and shuffled around like an object like a bird in a gilded cage. I had my privileges, but my world was still a prison. They hadn't even left me with a book to read, so I stared out the window until the jeeps veered off the main road and down a half-mile driveway, flanked by armed guards.

"Are all these guards for me?"

"They're a local security team," Mace replied, "More of a deterrent than anything. We're the real deal."

"Right. Will I get to shower here? Or have clothing?"

"Yes ma'am."

"When are we leaving for —"

"I can't disclose our location, ma'am. But you can guarantee we'll be departing tomorrow after dark."

Seeing that his responses had been less than satisfactory, Mace caught my eye in the rearview mirror.

"Sorry, Amy. I'm just following orders."

"Yeah. Wonderful."

"If I could tell you more, I would."

We stopped off inside and Tyrese pulled me aside to talk. He explained that the next day, I'd be escorted out of the house at 2100 hours. He asked me who I got along with the most and who I felt most comfortable with guarding my bedroom at night.

"Mace," I replied.

"Really?" Tyrese seemed surprised, "It isn't Zhang?"

I shook my head furiously.

"If you say so ma'am."

Tyrese led me out into the hallway, back with the other men and he began to explain where they'd be posted in the villa throughout the night. As he spoke, I noticed something missing. I grasped my hand and realized that it was gone. My diamond bracelet. Vasily got it for me, for my seventeenth birthday. I didn't bother bringing it up. I doubted the men who had mocked me for my ignorance would tolerate the fact that I'd lost a diamond bracelet. Over 14 carats of diamonds gone, and what's worse was I had no idea where Vasily was.

We hadn't said a proper goodbye and father had probably not even told him of his plans.

Would I see him again? Were all of them in danger?

Mace led me to my room. He noticed the sullen look on my face as we approached.

"What's wrong?"

"Nothing."

"You've been clutching your wrist for the past five minutes. Don't tell me nothing's wrong."

"It's stupid," I muttered.

"Tell me. If there's a problem, I can take it to Captain Lorde."

"No, really, it's nothing."

"Amy…"

"Fine. I lost my bracelet."

He tried to disguise a smirk. I could practically see the thoughts racing through his head. He thought I was foolish, frivolous, shallow — or worse.

"That's it?"

"It's a diamond bracelet. My brother gave it to me."

"Sounds expensive."

"It was expensive."

"It'll turn up."

"Where? We are trapped here on this stupid island. And — it's gone."

I didn't think I could cry over such a silly thing like a bracelet, but it all hit me at once. I was away from my father, away from everyone I knew, and I had nothing and no way of getting out. I knew that at thirty, I should have been able to do something besides cry, but I was too naive to see my way out of it. These six men were doing my father's bidding by kidnapping me, and if Papa wanted something, you could never convince him to do otherwise.

I cried. Tears spilled from my eyes and as I tried to stifle a sob, that only made it sound louder and heavier in my chest. Mace's expression went from disdain to surprise. The bracelet meant a lot to me, but it wasn't all that was on my mind. All my emotions hit me at once. Hard.

"I'm sorry. Y-you're right. It's stupid," I muttered.

Instead of mocking me, Mace put his hand on my shoulders at the top of the stairs and patted my back in a comforting sort of way.

"Hey, chin up, princess. If you don't find it, I'm sure your brother would replace it for you. I don't get the impression your family's hurting for cash."

"I may never see my brother again." My voice caught.

"Who said that? We're going to keep you safe, Amy. You don't have to worry about that."

"You all are keeping me safe, but what about Papa? What about Feodor? Vasily? Boris? Who will keep them safe?"

"I get the impression the Usmanovs do a fine job of protecting themselves."

My tears dried up and Mace made a surprising move. He

hugged me. At first, it was awkward and uncomfortable, the sort of uncertain hug you do when you see a long lost friend after a long time apart . Mace held me tighter, and I allowed myself to hug him back. My heart raced, faster and faster. My tears dried up, but not because I wasn't sad. His chest pressed up against mine, his arms holding onto me so tightly that I didn't think he'd let go and the solid wall of muscle that pressed up against me distracted me from my troubles and transported me from the fantasy world of my problems to the fact that I was right here in sunny Bermuda with a soldier comforting me.

My attention to how tightly he held me and to the perfect chiseled nature of his body caused me to pull away uncomfortably, and visibly shaken.

"Did I go too far?"

"No. I think I should go into my room."

I hadn't meant it to sound suggestive, or even sexy. After that hug, I could feel heat rising in my chest and the familiar tell-tale signs of desire pulsing just beneath my flesh. He stared at me with his stark, stern professionalism. He'd never break for a moment. He'd never let me know how he felt, even if it burned him up inside the way it did to me. I could tell from the way he'd lingered in that comforting embrace.

A man like Mace Harwood would never let it go too far. He might do his duty as a gentleman to comfort me but that stiff starched uniform that stood beneath him would hold back the rambunctious, passionate beast beneath it. I wanted to reach out and touch his chest, to reach into his shirt and finger his silver dog tags between my palms.

"I think that's a great idea," he replied, his bashfulness coloring his face.

But to feel bashful at all meant that he felt what I felt. And judging by the slow rising in the fabric of his pants that he attempted to conceal with his posture, he liked what he felt.

Mace pushed the door to the bedroom open. It was cool, breezy, with starched cotton and white linen scents filling the room. A reed diffuser spread jasmine through the room. Mace pulled the curtains from the floor to ceiling windows aside, letting breathtaking orange light through.

"It's beautiful," I murmured.

He grunted, but didn't respond, the tension only getting thicker as he crossed over to the door.

"Aren't you supposed to wait outside?"

"No ma'am. Not tonight."

"How am I supposed to change? Shower? Sleep?"

"I'll be here, awake. I'll turn around when you need me to ma'am."

"Okay," I responded.

Cheekily, and almost just to gauge his reaction, I unbuttoned my blouse slowly.

"Miss Usmanov!" He snapped.

"Yes?"

I kept worked on the buttons.

"What are you doing?"

"I'm taking my shirt off."

He turned around, facing away from me. I didn't stop until the loose blouse hung around my shoulders.

"Mace, I want you to turn around."

"Why?"

"You know why."

"I don't think this is appropriate Miss Usmanov."

"Oh, so no more Amy?"

I'd found a boldness that I'd never held onto before. Something about Mace emboldened me.

"Listen, put your shirt back on and I'll turn around."

"It is on."

"Button it up."

I gave an exasperated sigh and worked my buttons up all the way. Mace turned around just in time, a crazed look in his eye.

"What are you playing at?"

"Nothing."

"Is this a test? Are you trying to get me fired?"

He crossed the room, standing face to face with me, seething with anger.

"It wasn't a test!"

"I don't believe you," he snarled.

"It wasn't!"

"Then what on earth were you doing?"

He stared into my eyes and I stared into his. He'd seen unimaginable things, I could tell. Behind his tough exterior, behind his cold starched uniform, I knew there was a man too beautiful to touch. I longed to explore him, to discover the man behind the stiff rules.

"I made a mistake, I suppose."

He grabbed my arm.

"Why are you looking at me like that, then?"

"Because…"

He lifted my arm over my head slowly, and then grabbed the other one, raising them both over my head and rendering me immobile. He pinned both of my arms together and held them tightly with one hand.

"Let go of me!" I squealed.

"Why should I?"

"Because!"

"Do you think that's all men are worth? Jumping to your every command simply because you asked it?"

"That's not what—"

"If you'd tried those games with Chubb or Peña, they might have pushed you up against the wall, had their way with you."

"Let go of me!"

"Is that what you wanted?"

He stepped forward, I stepped back to counter him getting closer, my wrists still imprisoned by his forceful masculine grip.

"No!"

"Then why would you take your shirt off in front of a stranger?"

He stepped back again. I demanded again that he let go of me.

"Why would you show me that gorgeous satin red bra, cupping your perfect tits."

He'd looked. I couldn't figure out how but he'd taken a peek at what I tried to show him. I took another step back again and this time, he had me pressed up against the wall with my arms hovering over my head. He was in control of me. I couldn't move forward or backwards now. Wriggling in an attempt to leave his grasp would never work.

"Mace—"

"Shhh," he whispered, "I know you want this."

"I don't—"

"Yes you do. I bet if I stuck my hands down your pants they'd come back dripping wet."

"No—"

"Then tell the truth. Why did you show me your tits."

"I didn't—"

"Don't lie," he interrupted, "Tell the truth, Amy."

· · ·

I trailed off, hoping he wouldn't be so cruel as to make me say it and confess out loud what I wanted from him. He didn't loosen his grip on me even for a moment. He leaned in close, his other hand touching my waist for the first time. My panties were soaked, and a few drops of wetness began to trail down my thigh over the fleshy muscles and down my trembling calves.

"You wanted me to take you and fuck you. You don't want to admit it because you're a spoiled little rich girl, but that's what you wanted."

I could smell the bay rum on his neck, the starched material of his army uniform and then his intense, masculine musk penetrating through the fabric as he inched closer and closer to me.

He continued, "You wanted me to take my cock and stick it in your tight little pussy."

"No—"

"Admit it."

"I won't."

What I meant was, "I can't". I couldn't bring myself to beg for him. I couldn't bring myself to admit that more than anything, I wanted the strong soldier who had both violated me and protected me to take everything a step further. I couldn't admit that I wanted his rough hands down my panties, fondling my sopping pussy lips and sliding between my legs until I climaxed. I couldn't admit that out of all the men I'd met throughout my life, this stern, stoic soldier had what I desperately wanted and needed.

"Admit it," he repeated, "You want me to fuck you."

"No…"

"If you admit it, you just might get what you want, princess."

"What if we get caught?" I tried again to make another excuse, but I was weak and getting weaker as his body pressed up against mine and I could feel his abs and his cock, straining to get out of his blue camouflage uniform.

He leaned forward and kissed me for the first time. It was hot, wet, and hard, with his tongue pressing deep into my mouth. He pulled away just as I moaned into his lips.

"We won't get caught. I promise."

I couldn't stand it for another moment. From the second he kissed me, I had to have more. I couldn't live in denial again.

"Fine. I admit it. I want you to fuck me."

He pressed up against me closer again. His hand ran down from my neck, over the mound of my breasts, down my flat stomach and past the waistband of my pants. He slipped his rough hands past my underwear and dipped two fingers between my pussy lips.

"Just like I thought," he murmured, "You're soaked."

His fingers moved between my lips and he started to massage the soft pink folds between my legs. He moved his fingers slowly at first and then started to focus his attention on my clit. I could feel his manhood straining through his fatigues as he pressed me against the wall and worked his fingers against my clit. I gasped and wriggled, attempting to free myself from his grasp, but I found myself weak and pliable in his grip.

I moaned as he slipped one finger past my entrance and kept his body pressed against mine. He kissed me, leaning in to whisper in my ear as he held me up against the wall.

"I want to hear you ask for it again…"

"Please," I whimpered, "Fuck me…"

He removed his hardness from his fatigues, pulling his pants down just over his ass and slipping his cock out of his boxers. He kept me pinned against the wall with one hand and then used the other to get my pants down around my knees. Using his free hand, he lifted me off my feet and pressed me up against the wall. He positions his hardness at my entrance.

"I have nothing to worry about right?"

"No. I'm on the pill."

"Good."

He thrust his entire length in with one swift stroke. He split me open, spreading my tightness to its full capacity around his intense, throbbing cock. I moaned, unable to get free as he pounded into me, slamming me against the wall; my wetness dripped around his cock and my juices spilled down my thighs and over his tumescent member.

"Fuck me…" I moaned.

He pounded into me harder, and harder. I couldn't hold back. I released, climaxing over his cock and tilting my head back to expose my neck as I came. He leaned forward, wrapping his lips around a sensitive bit of flesh on my neck as I came all over him. As I came, he grunted, pounding into me harder and harder until he couldn't take it anymore and his thick cock exploded between my legs, coating the walls of my pussy and my thighs with spurts of his white seed.

I moaned and wrapped my legs around him, squeezing his cock deeper inside me as he finished and holding his firm body between my legs. Another climax ravaged my body as he finished inside me. By the time he pulled out, my legs were trembling. He let go of my arms and I wrapped them around his neck. He lifted me over to the bed and tossed me onto the mattress, his cum still leaking out of my pussy.

"Get dressed and ready for bed. You don't want anyone to find you like this."

Heat rushed to my cheeks. He dominated me completely, enticing me to submit to him and then following it up with the stoic aloofness he'd presented me earlier. But for a moment, in his arms, I'd seen his façade crack. I knew that beneath the stern expression and brief words, there was a man of passion. My unfettered lust for him could never be allowed to take over, but just for one night, I'd had him, and the warmth in my stomach sent me deep into an easy night's sleep.

In the morning, Mace shook me awake and ordered me to get dressed. I did, and when we walked downstairs to meet the rest of the team, heat rushed to my cheeks again. They were all acting normally, but I couldn't help but fear that my previous night's actions had been exposed. Tyrese Lorde commanded them to take me to the jeeps and we split up again. This time, Tyrese drove me himself. Despite what had happened with Mace, I was grateful. I didn't want to talk about what had happened between us.

We came to a dock on an isolated part of the island. We had

driven for five miles without seeing any other cars. When the men left the jeeps, they were armed. Tyrese led me to the foot of the dock where a boat waited. It looked like a decent sized fishing boat, smaller than the yacht Papa had chartered for our family vacations to Croatia, but big enough to have eight cabins.

"This will be our home for the next five days," Tyrese informed me.

I was tired of protesting. I had no choice in the matter and nothing that I said would change the fact that this team would get me onto that boat.

"Where are we going?" I asked, acknowledging the futility of my question.

"Far away."

"Will I meet Papa there?"

"No. And I'm sorry Miss Usmanov, but I've had enough of the questions."

Reluctantly, I boarded the ship. Chubb and Ellis led me to my private cabin with a bed, a side table and a small closet. They closed the door behind me and prepared the boat to leave shore. In the small closet next to my bed, I had winter clothing, boots, and underwear. Some of it I recognized, but most of it was new and slightly too large for me. On the bedside table, there was a copy of War And Peace, in Russian, that I recognized from Papa's personal library. I opened it and sure enough, there was an inscription from him.

"You'll be gone a long time. I miss you already, Milena. I hope one day you can forgive your old man — O."

Tears welled in my eyes. I wanted to throw the book against the wall but a scene might cause Chubb and Ellis to check on me, the last thing I wanted. I heard the motor roar to life and as I struggled to balance, I realized we were on the open ocean. I flopped back on my bed, waiting. I fingered the pages of Tolstoy's great work until I couldn't take him prattling any longer, and I shut the book and fell asleep.

The rocking boat woke me up and for a moment, I couldn't remember where I was. I heard the men screaming to each other and I sat up straight. The boat swayed like a cradle and I was as powerless as a newborn. If I rose, I would fall. A lump formed in my throat and I considered crying out for help, or at least to figure out what was happening. Before I could say anything, Mace thrust the door open, his eyes wide with terror. The thin light hanging above his head on the ceiling outside narrowly missed his skull as it swayed.

"We have a problem, Amy. I need you to come with me."

"What's happening?"

"Take my hand. Don't worry. It'll all be okay."

"Mace!"

"My hand!" He bellowed.

I'd never seen him like this. I reached forward. The boat rocked and he fell into my door frame. Regaining his balance, he reached for my hand again, this time catching it and squeezing me so tightly, I thought my bones were going to break. He pulled me out of the room but struggled to stand on his feet.

"We need to get above deck. The boat is sinking."

"Huh?"

Before I could get an answer, I noticed a ball of yellow light in my peripheral vision. I turned my neck and saw the swinging lightbulb coming straight for my face. Before I could call Mace's name, it hit my face, hard. For a split second, I thought I would be okay and then I collapsed on the ground. I only had another moment of consciousness, just enough for me to say one word, "Mace!"

Then that was it. I was out like a light, as my safe passage sank to the bottom of the sea.

Part II

※

MACE

She was wet. Soaked to the bone. And cold. Shit. I dragged her onto the shore and flicked open my watch compass. Co-ordinates. Quick calculations. Shit. We were something like 245 miles give or take a few away from the island where we should have landed. We'd decided to sail North to avoid hitting the storm but God had other plans and we strayed too far in the frozen Northern seas. If Ellis had more to drink maybe he would've steered us better. To avoid the seasickness, I'd had as much vodka as my stomach could fit and if it weren't for the liquor warming me off, I mightn't have made it to shore.

Hell, I didn't know if any of the men made it. My mission was to save Aminata, not them. To protect her. To keep her safe. I dragged her body to the shore and saw her dark lips a shade of even darker blue. I reached into my emergency kit for a blanket. To keep her warm I'd have to strip her naked. I pulled her up onto the sugary white sand and as the northern wind whipped all around me, chilling me to the bone, I got her naked and wrapped her in a hypothermia blanket. She was lightweight in my arms. As I wrapped her up, I realized how truly fragile she was. I stared out at the horizon. Something orange floated in the distance, nearly obscured by the snow and sand whipped up into a frenzy by the northern winds.

I pulled her away from the shore and noticed a thicket of dense pine trees a few hundred feet off. I'd have to carry her and make a fire. Quick. We didn't have long until the two of us would freeze to death. I grunted and hoisted her over my shoulder. She slumped over, still asleep. I hiked through the sand and then the knee deep snow to the clearing near the trees. I set her on the ground, propping her face up so it was out of the snow. I struggled to find tinder but desperation served me well and I worked up a big sweat as I built a fire. I scraped the sticks against each other, my bare fingers numb as I created friction. A tiny spark.

That was all it took and I nursed the fire until it roared. And I sat Aminata up against a large log I'd dragged over and I touched her cheek with my warmed hand. She was still cold. And sleeping. That light had hit her in the face pretty good and when I tossed her overboard into the raft, a large wave had washed over her, soaking her clean through. I lost track of Tyrese but he'd been waving his arms around like a maniac and barking orders at Zhang and Ellis to go wake Robbie, who had been particularly despondent since we'd left Bermuda on account of some news about his kids. I didn't know if any of the men made it and as the sky darkened, I knew if they didn't get to shore, they wouldn't have long.

Chubb came through the woods first, soaking wet and clutching his stomach praying for God's forgiveness with blubbering blue lips until he saw my fire and he fell to his knees, a bit delirious from the cold. I passed him my flask of vodka, which had luckily survived the crash and he dribbled it down his lips. I hid my annoyance at the wastage, giving him a terse smile as he settled in front of the fire. He was a strong man who had served a couple tours of duty and despite his blubbering, he bounced back quick. Lorde and Zhang were the next two to arrive. Zhang carried the captain over his shoulder and as he sat Tyrese down in front the fire, he mentioned calmly that Tyrese had hit his head on the way down and as he'd gone to rescue him, he'd obtained a slight scratch.

Zhang's leg had been impaled by a sharp metal spike that luckily hadn't passed more than two inches into his flesh. Chubb had more medical training than I did so he patched him up as I wandered back out of the protective shelter of the woods to the shore one more time. Zhang had been nursing his own flask of rum, and as I walked to shore, more of our emergency packs had floated up against the sand. Avoiding the waves, I rushed to the shore and pulled the packs up. One of them had liquor. Thank God for that. We had two days of emergency rations. As I pulled up some of the emergency shelters, I noticed a head bobbing in the cold water. And then another.

Ellis and Robbie, both swimming towards shore. They must've paddled as close as they could get and capsized their lifeboat. I waved to them and called and they didn't respond. The water was too cold for them to survive more than five minutes beneath the surface and when they got to shore they stripped down to nothing and unwrapped their vacuum sealed hypothermia blankets, wrapping their bodies tightly.

"I got a fire," I told them, "Get to the woods."

They nodded and ran as fast as their legs could take them. When Ellis collapsed to his knees, Robbie picked him back up and the two of them cursed and howled as each other miserably as I followed with nearly 100lbs of supplies on my back. I grunted as I set all the supplies on the ground. By then, Tyrese was awake. Chubb figured that Tyrese had a concussion, but our Captain still had his head on well enough to bark orders at us. He cared more for Aminata's well being than ours. He had Robbie and Tim Zhang set up her tent. After that we moved her in with the emergency fleece blankets we had that were lucky enough to wash up on shore. Prioritizing the heiress meant that a couple of us came up short on supplies. Lorde made Peña and Chubb share a tent, then assigned me to the tent with Tim Zhang and Bubba Ellis. He'd join Peña and Chubb but of course, someone would have to sit and watch Aminata's tent at night. We had to take shifts — two shifts alternating every 12 hours so that each of us would have a couple days rest.

She hadn't roused yet, but before she did, Tyrese warned us to put on a good face about everything.

"We've got two days of supplies here, and we will be waiting for rescue for nearly eight days."

"Eight days?!"

"If not longer," Tyrese replied, glowering at Chubb for daring to say something that sounded too close to a complaint.

"I'll need you boys to man up. We have a woman to protect and we will be investigating this crash as soon as we return to American soil. For now we have one goal: survival."

"Why do we have to wait so long for help?" Zhang asked.

"The storm. Radio has been knocked out. I managed to send out an S.O.S. But we won't know if they've received it for a while."

"Is the girl awake?" Robbie asked.

"Nah. Still sleeping," Chubb replied, "I bet she'll lose her mind when she sees where we are."

Tyrese glowered and sneered, "None of you are to do anything but make her stay here entirely comfortable. She says to jump, you ask how high? Her father is one of the most powerful men in Russia and if one hair on his daughter's head is harmed, he will be out for blood."

"We can't help the crash!" Robbie countered.

"Yeah, but there's a chance it might've been foul play," I replied.

Tyrese raised an eyebrow.

"What makes you say that?"

"The rig. I checked it out myself before we got her. There were no problems. We should have been able to sail clean around that iceberg."

"We didn't *hit* an iceberg," Robbie replied.

"Then what happened?" Tyrese retorted.

"No sé," Robbie replied with a shrug.

"I'm hungry," Ellis remarked, changing the subject now that all of us had feeling restored to our extremities.

"We got enough rations for two days," Chester said, gesturing to the packages that survived our crash.

"We'll have to hunt," Zhang suggested.

"Right. I checked the co-ordinates and this island has wolves, a species of brown bear, some small game and geese as well as a few sea birds. Either that or it's totally desolate. Without better equipment, I can't tell."

"Any deer?" Chester asked.

He'd been an expert game hunter down in Georgia during his heyday.

"You boys will have to find out and tell me. Peña, Zhang, Chubb, you take the Western side of the island. I'll head out with Ellis and explore the East."

"Boss?" I asked.

"Stay with the lady. She seems to have taken a liking to you for whatever reason."

"As long as y'all leave the booze with me, I'm good."

"Try not to drown yourself in it," Tyrese remarked snidely.

I grinned and took a cheeky swig from my flask, causing Tyrese to glower in disdain while the rest of the fellas snickered. They spread out with hunting knives and weapons. Not much survived the crash. One shotgun, a few knives, a small machete and an axe. I unzipped Aminata's tent and crawled inside where she lay with a blanket wrapped around her.

"Aminata," I whispered, seeing if it would rouse her.

It didn't work at first, so I sat up straight and waited for her to get up. Lying there just waiting would have been boring if I didn't have enough liquor on me to get a whale drunk. When she finally stirred, I was red in the face and I stank like vodka.

"Is that vodka?" She whispered.

Her voice startled me, as it came a whisper in the darkness and I hardly noticed it at first until she said it again.

"You awake?"

"Vodka. I can smell it."

"Sorry—"

"No. I need some."

I shuffled over to where she was sleeping, my eyes had adjusted to the darkness, but I could still only make out her shadow. I touched her arm and she sat up, the blanket falling away from her chest as I tipped the flask of vodka to her lips. She drank. And drank. And drank. I had the feeling that she could out drink even Ellis. She smacked her lips once she finished.

"Ah. Good."

She looked down and noticed her exposed breasts, a confused expression crossing her face.

"Why am I naked? Where am I?"

"We're off the boat."

"I gathered."

"There was a storm. The boat capsized. I got you outta there."

"The rest of them?"

"They're fine. We're SEAL's. This is a walk in the park."

"A walk in the park you say? Does that have anything to do with why I'm naked?"

"No. You nearly got hypothermia from the water after you passed out. I had no choice. I'm sorry."

"I guess it's old news to you."

"No. It's not like that, Amy."

"Can a girl get a t-shirt over here?"

"Sure. I've got a sweater and some pants. They may be a little big, but it'll keep you from dying of exposure."

I tossed her a fleece sweater and skintight fleece leggings. She shimmied into them both and then she curled her knees up all the way to her chest.

"Where are we?"

"I don't know."

"This wasn't where we were supposed to land?"

"No."

"Is help on the way?"

"Not for a while."

"Mace… How could something like this happen? Is this common or something?"

"No. It's not. Tyrese says we'll have to investigate."

"I have a bad feeling about this."

For a woman who snubbed her father's paranoia about what

would happen to her, the concern struck me. I had to do what was in my power to comfort her, I knew that.

"Listen, Amy," I whispered, reaching out to hold her hand, "I promise we won't let anything happen to you. We're here to keep you safe."

"You can't stop me from starving to death if we run out of food."

"That's why the guys are hunting. I promise, we'll look after you."

"Does anyone know about us?" She asked, another question popping into her mind, evidently.

"No," I whispered, squeezing her hand just a bit.

"Good. I don't know how to explain it but… I don't really want to talk about it."

"Shit, we don't have to talk."

"You're right," she nodded, "More vodka?"

Was it possible for me to fall in love with a woman this fast? She took my flask before I could even say yes and she tilted it back into her mouth, finishing the last drop.

"Americans. You have such weak vodka."

"We might have weak vodka, but we make strong whiskey."

"Oh yeah?"

"I can prove it to you."

"I'm not interested. I'd rather you…" she touched her fingertips to my chest, "I'd rather you keep me warm tonight."

"Are you sure that's a good idea?"

"I'm sure that it isn't."

I kissed her. I couldn't help it. Her smooth, sultry voice and her hands touching my chest reminded me of what heaven I'd unleashed by diving between her milky thighs. I had to have her again. No part of me could resist spreading those legs apart and this time perhaps, tasting her.

"The men could come back at any minute," I whispered to her, giving her a chance to back out.

After all we'd been through, if she unleashed the animal within me there was no telling how wild I could get. Liquor and sex were my two coping mechanisms and I'd had just enough liquor to remove every last one of my inhibitions about nailing her.

"I don't care," she replied, "I'll have to be quiet."

I couldn't help but flash her my signature Harwood smirk.

"You and I both know that you won't be quiet."

She gave me that sexy little "shut up and kiss me" look and I had no choice but to oblige. I clutched the small of her back as it expanded in slow, shuddering breaths that trembled as her arousal heightened. My lips moved from hers down to her neck. She tilted her neck to the side, some of her damp hair tickling my face and sending surges of arousal coursing through me. I heard a wolf howl in the distance, a sound terrifying and primal, and one that I was grateful she'd missed. I slipped the fleece off of her and she shivered. It was cold... too cold. The temperature would only drop overnight and tomorrow, no one could predict what weather we would face. She wore no bra beneath her shirt. Her nipples stood hard at attention from the moment they were exposed.

I love a pair of beautiful bouncing tits like hers. I leaned forward and took one nipple into my mouth as my fingers caressed and pinched the second one. She moaned as my soft warm tongue touched her hardened nipple. So much for keeping things quiet. She couldn't help herself and she moaned again when I moved to the other nipple and unconsciously spread her legs apart, inviting me to move closer between her legs so that the warmth of her tight heat emanating from the fleece leggings may entice me to go further. Her thighs pressed up against my torso and desire made me weak.

I grabbed madly for her pants and slipped her out of them. Again, she wore no underwear, giving me easy access to the space between her thighs which sat flushed, engorged and drooling with her love honey. She spread her thighs apart another inch and a sticky smacking sound emanated through the tent. If she were any wetter, I might've drowned. I pushed her onto her back and positioned my head between her thighs. Her knees pointed to the roof of the tent and trembled slightly from the cold as I worked my way between her legs. I could have my way with her now, and I knew it. No part of her would resist once she was like this, sitting in perfect surrender in my grasp. I ran my tongue along the length of her outer pussy lips and she moaned, arching her back and raising her toes just an inch off the ground.

I ran my tongue along the length of her wetness again, and then stroked it all the way back, allowing my tongue to touch her tenderest hole. She arched her buttocks up and I squeezed the cheeks, pulling her deeper into my mouth like a tender, juicy, peach. I slipped one of my fingers between her legs and began moving them against the fleshy pad of her wetness. She cried out as I massaged the tender spot between her legs and my tongue continued to work her wetness.

Her hands ran through my hair, tickling my scalp. I thrust my tongue and fingers deeper between her legs. She moaned as I drove my fingers deeper and unlocked the explosive pleasure centers between her legs. She came. Hard. I squeezed her thighs between my fingers steadying her as her body shook with pleasure. She moaned my name in that soft, sexy little voice of hers.

"Mace…"

I pulled my face away from her wetness and stared down at her as her chest heaved and her thighs lay splattered with a mixture of her juices. Everything about her was pure performance art. I kneeled between her legs and removed my shirt. Amy craned her neck upwards to catch a glimpse of the view. Civilians all reacted the same way to the raw, chiseled bodies of America's finest in the navy. Every inch of my body was covered in thick, sinewy muscles, from my gleaming thick pectorals all the way down to the perfect v-shape that guided her eye from my glistening abs to my rock hard cock, currently tucked inside my freshly dried uniform.

With my shirt off, she sat up and reached out to touch my abs. Her warm hands stroked the dips and curves of my muscles until she got to my pants. She fumbled with the button until I firmly moved her hand away.

"Patience," I demanded.

I loved making her wait. I enjoyed every moment of teasing her and titillating her until she had no choice but to succumb completely to her wanton desires. I started with my pants slowly. Her tongue bolted out of her mouth and licked her lips quickly and subconsciously. My manhood rose in my pants, bursting through the thick camouflage fabric ready to meet her head on. I peeled my pants down just over my hips. My thighs muscles flexed in anticipation, each of my muscles bulging as hot desire flowed through the fleshy staff between my legs.

Aminata was practically drooling with desire.I couldn't contain my desire. I pulled my pants down and then my boxers. By the time I exposed my throbbing cock to the cool air in the tent, my need to tease Aminata had diminished. All I wanted now was to drive my staff between her legs and plunge into her until both of us shook from the force of a powerful climax.

I lined my bare cock up against her tight entrance which continued to ooze with her creamy juices. Before sliding inside her, I leaned over and pushed the hair out of her face, stroking her cheek with my warm hand. I kissed her and she kissed back hard, pushing her tongue down my throat and tasting the vodka on my lips.

"Am I too drunk to do this?" I asked, the liquor hitting me different and causing woozy uncertainty to fog through my head.

"No," she whispered, "I want you."

We were drunk on each other's skin and nothing could have pulled either of us away from the edge. I slipped the bursting head on my engorged dusky pink cock past her entrance. Only an inch was enough to drive her mad. She moaned and spread her legs wider, the flesh of her entrance gripping tightly around the invading head of my cock. I thrust another inch between her legs. She cried out again, arching her back upward so she enveloped another few inches of my hardness. Her wetness gripped me tighter and fitting the remaining inches inside her became more difficult. I grunted and thrust again, this time burying my full length inside her dripping wet honeypot.

"Harder," she whimpered.

I had barely buried my length between her legs but she already mewed and squealed for more. Placing my hands on her hips, I slid out of her wetness and then cut through the depth fo it with a long, deep stroke. She moaned as I drove my cock deep between her legs and she exploded with an earth-shattering climax as my full-length lay deep between her legs. Slow strokes heat her body up slowly until she burned like a furnace beneath my fingers and as I drove into her harder and deeper she couldn't help but cum loudly. As she moaned, her nails dug into my back, clawing at my muscles and sinewy flesh. As my back muscles flexed, she only drew closer to a climax.

"Ohhh," she cried out, "Yes, Mace, yes…"

Keeping quiet was off the table now. She dragged her nails down my spine and then pulled my taut ass cheeks deeper between her legs. As she pushed my cock to new depths, she came again and her pussy tightening around my cock pushed me close to the brink. I pulled out of her swiftly and flipped her onto her stomach. The arch of her back where her firm, toned buttocks curved like a hillside created the perfect shape, enticing me to drive my cock into her.

I spread her ass cheeks apart, exposing that tiny hole that

concealed the entrance to her depths. Her tight hole shuddered and juices leaked out in anticipation as my fingers explored and examined the flesh surrounding Amy's perfect tight spot. I placed the head of my cock at her entrance and she wriggled her ass cheeks. I thrust deep between her legs and as she moaned, I plunged between those thighs deeper and harder. From this angle, I smacked against her soft, fleshy ass cheeks and my cock dove deeper between her pussy lips, taking every last inch of her perfect flesh for mine. I spread her ass cheeks apart, allowing my cock to drive deeper inside her. She came again, loudly. As she moaned, I couldn't help but draw close to an incredible climax of my own. She arched her back and I pounded away faster and faster. As she came for the last time, I couldn't help myself. I grunted and exploded, pulling my cock out of her wetness just in time and erupting with my thick white fluids all over her ass. She moaned as I pulled out of her and her skin responded to my touch as my cum coated her ass and I tapped my dick against her cheeks, causing them to jiggle. As I pulled away from her, we heard men's voices.

"They're coming," she said sharply.

The two of us couldn't have covered up the scene any faster. We disposed of all evidence that we'd had an erotic encounter and shimmied back into our clothing. The tent was warm now and the scent of sex and of body parts mashing together in bliss filled the tiny cavern.

"We'd better go out by the fire," I told her.

"Think they found food?" She asked.

"I hope so," I murmured.

I'd worked up a big appetite and without food, we would be in big trouble out here in the wilderness.

She left the tent first and I followed, sitting next to her on a log next to the fire. The fire had subsided significantly since the men's departure so I added more kindling to enhance the flames and disguise the fact that I'd ignored tending it for so long while we made love. By the time Tyrese stormed out of the thicket into the clearing, there were no signs that we had done anything but sit and diligently wait for their return. Tyrese had four rabbits slung over his shoulder. Aminata wrinkled her nose when she saw them, but despite her initial misgivings, there was no choice.

The rest of the men returned with equally small game. Tyrese had cleaned the rabbits, and he left the rest of the men to take care of a small wild pig that Tim Zhang caught. While they cleaned the meat, Tyrese cut up the rabbits and made skewers with them. If we could save our rations for a true emergency, that would be the best way. Tyrese served us all and we cracked open a bottle of liquor.

I'd already stored a handle of vodka away for emergencies, but that left us plenty of American whiskey and some Scotch as well as a small bottle of Cognac. Tyrese insisted we open the cognac and we washed down our rabbit meat with small sips, passing the bottle around the group until we'd eaten our belly full. Tyrese gave the rabbit furs to Chubb for him to clean. He knew what to do to turn those furs into something wearable to cut down on our exposure to the elements. But that would be tomorrow's work. The sun had gone down and with wolves and bears in the wood, it weren't too safe to wander far from camp.

After we ate, we buried the stores of meat in the snow, deep enough that it would freeze. Ellis took the bones a few hundred feet away from camp and buried them too. Chubb cleaned the furs as best he could and hung them from tall tree branches.

Tyrese commanded Zhang to take first watch, and I volunteered to take second. The rest of the men were more than happy that the two of us had claimed the first night. Aminata retired to bed as soon as she could. I hated separating from her, even if it was for a few hours. I slept as much as I could and early in the morning, just after sunrise, I changed guard with Zhang and allowed him to get some sleep. To keep busy, I drank vodka and turned over scenes between myself and Amy in my mind.

That woman was something. She shared my passion for vodka, but without all the darkness that came with it. She had that gorgeous smile and that wild-eyed look whenever she stumbled upon the idea to do something that she knew she shouldn't be doing, like making love to me. I couldn't stand not being able to sneak in there and touch her. I want to press my hand to her mouth to quiet her down and slip her out of those clothes, pressing my cock into her one more time before the men woke up.

Tyrese rousing early woke me out of my deep fantasy about her.

"You good?" He asked.

"Yes, sir."

"You're handling this well, Mace."

"I ain't got a choice, sir. Missions go wrong all the time."

Tyrese nodded and sat next to me on the log that I'd dragged outside the front of Amy's tent.

"Tell me something, Mace. You checked the boat yourself?"

"Yes, sir. You read my report. This ain't my first rodeo."

"It's strange, don't you think."

"Yes, sir."

"Can I be straight with you, Mace?"

"Yes, sir."

The two of us had served tours together long before we met any of the men who had been assigned this mission. I knew Tyrese Lorde better than I knew most other SEALs. Any man I knew better than him had already died in some godforsaken Middle Eastern desert, or had been blown up by mines in Siberia or Chechnya.

"As soon as you said you suspected foul play, I knew you were onto something that I didn't want to admit. Our team is supposed to be close. We're a brotherhood. We've sworn loyalty to the flag and to our country."

"Yes, sir."

"I've poured over these men's service records myself. Nothing has suggested something as serious as treason. Nothing has suggested that any of these men would risk the lives of the rest of us for any reason."

"Maybe it wasn't about us… but about her."

"Someone out for the Russians?" Tyrese asked, considering my theory seriously.

"Her father said she was in grave danger. But he didn't specify from who."

Tyrese shrugged and replied, "If my sources are correct, Oleg Usmanov has many enemies. Up until recently, the man I owed this favor, Oliver Cook, would have considered himself one of those enemies."

"The Russians don't play nice. They never have," I reminded him.

We'd been in conflicts with the Russians before and I didn't have to remind Tyrese that Russians didn't have to be mobsters to play rough.

"Exactly. But to try to kill six Navy SEALs… Whoever this is must have nuts of steel."

"We won't be able to know for sure until we get back to American soil," I reminded him.

Tyrese snorted.

"Yeah, if any of us make it back."

"Do you think whoever has done this has more in store for us?"

"We were sunk just close enough to this island. I don't think it was an accident."

"I'll keep my eyes open, Cap."

"Good. I know you aren't my first officer, but I trust you with my life, Harwood."

"I respect that sir. Want a sip?"

Tyrese wrinkled his nose.

"It's dawn, boy. Put the liquor away and set an example for the other men."

"Sorry. It's those cold nights. They get to you."

Tyrese didn't react. He wanted his orders followed and that was that.

"Just get rid of the liquor, Mace. I don't want any more trouble, especially not from you."

AMINATA (AMY)

Tyrese forbade the men from having me lift a finger. After we were all awake, he went off in search of water and had Robbie Peña, the short Latino one, and Ellis, the tall Germanic looking one make breakfast. We had powdered eggs from their rations and then more skewers of rabbit meat. It was hardly gourmet, but the best I could expect under the circumstances. Mace sat next to me on the log, but I was afraid to speak to him in front of the others in case they figured out that something had gone on between us.

His poker face was better than mine. As the men cleaned up, they started drinking, especially on account of Tyrese being gone to search for water. They all sat around passing down a bottle of whiskey and their stories got as wild as their stench did. Mace was the only one who avoided sharing their bottle as he had his own bottle of vodka that he'd been nursing quite fiercely the whole night if my observations were correct.

Chubb got up and swiped the flask of vodka from Mace's hand.

"Stop hogging the flask."

Mace glowered and rose to his feet.

"Are you trying to fight, Chubb?"

"You're so drunk I could take you out with my finger."

"Wanna bet?"

"What's going on Harwood? Trying to impress the lady over here? I didn't peg you for a nigger lover."

I furrowed my brow in confusion. What had he just called Mace? I'd never heard the phrase in my life but judging by Mace's strong response, it meant something really bad. Mace grabbed onto Chester's collar, pulling the man up off the ground an inch.

"You watch your fuckin' mouth."

"Or what?"

"Hey man, calm down," Peña tried to calm in with his soft-spoken voice.

Ellis chuckled, "Let 'em handle their fight on their own."

Zhang said nothing. He sat in the corner eating quietly.

"I will knock your jaw out if you call me that again or if you call her that word."

"What word?" Chubb replied with a shit eating grin.

"You know what word…" Mace snarled.

"What? A nigger?"

Mace grunted and pushed Chester back. Before Chester

could gain his balance properly, Mace landed a sharp right hook at the man's cheek. That was all it took. Once he threw the first punch, Chester felt completely justified in fighting back. He threw a kick, which Mace dodged and then lunged at him with his full weight. Knocking Mace to the ground in a football tackle, for a moment Chester appeared to have the upper hand. Mace pushed him over and straddled him, pinning Chester to the ground with his thighs as he raised his fists and hit the man in the face again.

"Bastard! You apologize!" Mace yelled.

With reddened cheeks, it was clear that the liquor he'd consumed had plenty to do with his response.

"Nigger, nigger, nigger!" Chester bellowed, pushing Mace to go further and continue lobbing blows at Chester's head which he did his best to avoid while blood spilled out of his nose. By then, I understood what they were fighting about. I was too scared to get involved, so I stared at the fire, or looked over at the other men to see if any of them would step in and pull the men off each other.

For a moment, I had the morbid thought that they were hoping one of them would die because maybe we were low on rations and one more person would only make it harder to survive. A lump formed in my throat as the terror washed over me.

At this point, Peña screamed at Zhang, "Do something man! These idiots are gonna kill each other."

"They won't," Zhang said simply, and he resumed picking his rabbit meat off the bone.

Ellis barked, "C'mon fellas, pack it in. Tyrese will kill us all if he finds y'all like this."

Mace landed another punch in Chester's face but he'd waited too long to give in to Ellis and Peña's requests to calm down. Tyrese emerged from the woods holding large water bladders, a vein popping out from his forehead the moment he witnessed the tomfoolery that had unfurled in his absence up close.

"HEY!" Tyrese barked, "What the hell is going on here!"

Tyrese's yell snapped Mace out of the trance that kept his fists slamming into Chester's face. He stood there, dumbfounded at his own actions.

"I want the two of you to get down and give me 500!"

"What is this, boot camp?" Chubb sneered.

"Do it now Officer Chubb. We have to maintain order and discipline out here or none of us will make it. So do what I say. NOW!"

Tyrese didn't have to bark his orders again. The two dropped down, bare palms in the snow and began to count. Tyrese turned his attention to Zhang, Peña, and Ellis, chiding all of them for standing by and watching the fight happen. After thoroughly lambasting them all, the men finally finished their pushups. Covered in sweat, and looking meaner than ever, Mace asked if he could go off to hunt. Tyrese nodded and took his shift guarding my tent. Inside, I wished that I had something to read. The copy of the novel Papa had given me, or preferably my cellphone with my social media feeds and text messages. I just had to wait. I listened to the men, who in Mace's absence lost interest in the fight, as they told jokes amongst each other and passed around more liquor. Every once in a while, Tyrese's voice would come through the tent and he'd ask, "Is everything alright Miss Usmanov."

It sounded dreadfully formal, but I appreciated his inquests into my wellbeing. It didn't take long for me to fall asleep. When I woke up, it was still daylight. I listened for the voices heard Peña, Chubb and Ellis. Tyrese and Tim Zhang must have still been gone. I huddled in the tent beneath the blankets and waited, hoping that Mace or Tyrese or Zhang would return soon. Those three I liked. Peña made me uncomfortable, but not in the same was that Chester and Bubba did. There was something cruel about their faces, like what they'd seen in war time had sapped the real man out of them and they were merely shadows of their former selves.

Boots crunched through the snow and the zipper to my tent arched before me and opened the tent door.

"Come on out," Bubba Ellis ordered.

His breath stank like liquor and beer. His cheeks were red, either from the cold or the drink. I couldn't tell which.

"No."

"Come on out little miss. We want to talk to you."

He broke from his tough voice a bit and chuckled. The laugh unnerved me more than his request. I didn't believe that I had much of the choice to deny him, so I slipped into my boots and stood out in the open air. As the day went on, the temperature warmed up just enough that my lips and ears didn't instantly freeze.

Peña sat off in the corner, sullen, like he didn't want anything to do with what was happening. Ellis and Chubb stood arm to arm with their arms folded. For a split second, the thought crossed my mind that I was at their mercy, and while they might have been trustworthy enough for a short trip, those men could also be very dangerous. If what I'd overheard was true and Tyrese suspected foul play, it was possible that the two men he'd left to guard me had been involved.

"Miss Usmanov," Chester started, "Mr. Ellis and I have a few questions about your story."

Their visible drunkenness caused the words to slur out of his mouth as slow as molasses. His tongue lolled about causing his speech to emerge in an unforgiving drawl.

Bubba Ellis continued where his partner left off.

"We've come to suspect that this boat crash wasn't an accident at all."

Chester continued, "We have reason to believe it was foul play."

Peña chimed in noncommittally from his seat, "I told you two this wasn't going to work."

"Quiet, beaner," Ellis snapped.

Chester kept his attention focused on me as he completed his accusation.

"We have no proof that you are who you say you are. When you think about it, your story does sound a little far fetched."

Ellis jumped in, seemingly giddy with excitement, as if he'd solved a big mystery, "What type of sense does it make for a Russian oligarch to have a daughter black as charcoal? He must've taken us for a fool and sent you on a mission under false pretenses."

Before allowing me a chance to contribute a single word, Chester continued to expand upon their theory.

"You are a Russian operative and you've brought us here so you can extract America's secrets and take them back to Putin or whichever commie motherfucker you work for," he asserted proudly.

"She won't admit it, even if it's true," Peña called.

Chester and Bubba grinned, wide unnerving grins that made the Cheshire cat's smile look genuine.

"We got ways of making people talk. Even brainwashed Russian spies."

"I'm not a spy!" I replied, taking my chance during the one moment of silence they'd allowed.

"Give it up, Aminata, if that's even your real name. We'll figure this out, one way or another, with or without your co-operation. Ellis, get the the poker."

Bubba Ellis strode over to the fire and pulled out a large stick with metal bent around the tip, glowing red hot. Their makeshift torture device released thick plumes of steam. Oh God, no. My stomach dropped. These men would have to be insane to use this on me, especially after Tyrese's warning not to harm a hair on my head. They couldn't be that insane, could they?

"Stop!" I called, "Don't come any closer to me with that thing."

"Tell us your real name!" Chester Chubb bellowed, red in the face.

"My name is Milena Aminata Usmanov. My father is Oleg

Usmanov. I have three brothers, Feodor, Boris and Vasily," I said, holding my voice steady as I spoke, hoping it would increase their belief in my story and stop the two of them before it was too late.

Bubba took a step closer to me, a grin illuminating his cerulean eyes. They were as icy and cold as our surroundings. He could do this remorselessly I realized, especially if he believed that doing so would be serving his country.

"I promise you, I am who I say I am!" I said, my voice getting high and desperate.

Bubba held the poker up, the orange glow illuminating his face in a gaunt, hellish appearance.

"We'll see about that…"

"HEY! HEY! ELLIS YOU PUT THAT DOWN!" Tim Zhang's voice sounded loud across the clearing. It was the loudest and the most that I'd heard him talk. He was red in the face, but sober, and without Tyrese at his side. On hearing his Commander's orders, Ellis dropped the poker into the snow and the glow was dampened and steam sizzled up in a thicker white plume.

"What the hell do you think you were doing? Tim Zhang asked, returning to his low, stern voice.

"N-nothing boss," Chester interjected.

"She's a Russian spy," Ellis replied, sticking to their lie, "We was only trying to find out what she knew."

"If Captain Lorde knew what you were doing…"

"Prove to us she's not a spy!" Ellis remarked.

"Do you really think the Captain would have gone on this mission unless he was absolutely sure of her identity? Or do you mean to tell me that you think Tyrese Lorde is a fool."

Both men were quiet, and embarrassed. An overindulgence of liquor had given them unfounded bravery which Tim quickly dissected with the slightest injection of logic.

"You two get out of here and wash your faces. I won't bother telling Tyrese about this, but you'd better toe the line the rest of the time we're here. Is that clear?"

"Yes, sir," they chimed together.

Tim approached me once they turned tail and returned to the woods.

"Are you okay?"

"Yeah. I am."

"Good. Captain will be back soon. Do you mind keeping this quiet? I know they're idiots, but they were drunk and they'll never do it again."

"No problem," I replied, "Thank you for stepping in there are the right time."

"That's my job, ma'am."

Tim bowed respectfully and then went over to talk to Peña, likely giving him the same spiel. Within a few moments of that conversation, Mace emerged from the woods. He locked eyes with me, but Zhang interrupted him before he could go over to me. They spoke in hushed, low tones and stopped talking once Tyrese emerged from the woods. He could sense something had happened, but none of the men were talking.

Mace's hunt had been successful and he'd foraged some greens and mushrooms to go along with the pork belly and remaining food that we had. The search for fresh food, and some plant with a promise of vitamin C, occupied most of their time during the day. Having spent all day alone in the woods, Mace was in a considerably better mood too.

After dinner, Tim took first watch, a move that I was most grateful for. He sat just outside the tent, poking his head in every once in a while. But he didn't speak. I tried to get some sleep during Tim's shift which I was grateful for because Mace's voice roused me out of my sleep in the middle of the night. There were no other sounds except the crackle of the fire, and his voice. I roused grumpily to find him unzipping my tent and climbing inside.

"Mace!" I hissed.

"Shh," he murmured, "They're all drunk as skunks and fast asleep."

"Even Tim?"

"I think he's drunker then the rest of them. Asian glow and all. He's been out for hours."

"Did you hear about what happened today?" I whispered to him.

He nodded and grabbed my hands, warming them between his thick palms.

"I heard. I weren't too happy about it."

"They think I'm not who I say I am."

"They're idiots," Mace whispered.

"I don't want to get hurt, Mace. I'm scared."

"Amy, you can't keep being scared."

I hadn't expected that response from him. I didn't like it at first. I had no choice but to be afraid. Everything I knew had been uprooted before me and my entire life had been built around a lie and around the man I thought my father was. Mace wanted me to move past my fear, but how could I when I barely understood what and who I should be careful of.

"I am scared. And I can't help it."

"I haven't let anything happen to you yet, have I?"

"You aren't always there," I replied.

"But be strong as if I am. Because I promise you, Amy, I'll never be more than just around the corner."

My mouth hung open, stunned. He grabbed the small of my back and leaned in to kiss me. I was numb. He pulled away with a confused look on his face.

"What's wrong?"

"You're being… intense."

"Is it too much?"

"No," I whispered, "It makes me want to live… to be wilder, more free, less afraid."

"You can be all of that, Aminata."

He kissed me again and this time I was more accepting of his lips against mine.

"I don't think I've felt this way about another woman," he whispered.

I couldn't really believe that. Not then. I had feelings for him too that were stronger than I imagined I could feel for a man that I'd only known a few days. The magnetism was only a part of it.

"Why do I feel like I've known you my whole life?" I whispered, touching my finger to his lips.

He stared back at me, his lips holding back everything he wanted to say and do to me, but just barely.

"I have no clue. It's… unbelievable."

"Kiss me again, please," I whispered.

The longer we talked, the less time we would have between the sheets together and that was the very last thing I wanted to sacrifice. Before anyone woke up, before the howling of wolves sent a ripple of unease throughout the camp, I had to feel Mace Harwood's body pressed against mine. The tent had already filled with his musk. I kissed him again and as his pheromones wafted straight to my brain, the wild lust I felt for him suddenly magnified. I reached for his shirt to tear it off. He'd already raised the fabric over his head so my nails clawed at his bare, muscular chest first. He liked when I got wild and he tossed his shirt across the tent and then grabbed the small part of my waist, squeezing it with a firm masculine grip.

I spread my legs wide around his torso as he lay me on my back and nibbled at my flesh as he alternated between his lips and his tongue, dragging them across my neck. I moaned and squeezed my thighs around his torso, holding him still. Mace never tired of giving. He lifted my shirt over my belly button and trailed kisses all the way down to my mound which quivered in remembrance of the last time his tongue made the daring journey between my legs. I'd cum so hard that I saw stars. He could make a woman crazy with his tongue, and he relished pushing me to the edge of glory and then teasing me until my release sat firmly in his control.

His dominance made sense given his military background. But in the bedroom he was all roughness and brute strength with none of the discipline that restrained him. Untamed love-making was different and uninhibited. I never once had to be the oligarch's daughter, or fulfill the role of the precious princess diplomat. He craved unlocking my inner goddess, the pure sensitive love-filled being that trembled in climax at the slightest touch. He lived to draw the darkness out of me.

His lips quickly found my entrance and he stroked between my lips and then pushed two of his fingers deep inside my entrance. I cried out loudly as he stretched me out and pleasured the most forbidden parts of my wetness. I hadn't expected him to bring me so close to climax so quickly. He'd revved me up in record time. I gasped and ran my hands over his hair, which had grown out longer and slightly thicker even in three days or so we had been traveling together. As I held his face between my legs, he only gripped my thighs tighter and began moving his lips faster and faster between my thighs. He nibbled on my outer lips before thrusting his powerful tongue between my legs and flicking it around my engorged clit. He was merciless and resisting intense climax was futile. My body trembled against my will as I reached an earth-shattering release. I cried out and threw my head back against the soft bedding beneath me, stifling my moans of pleasure. With all the men sleeping only a few feet away, I worried about waking any of them up.

After I came a few times, Mace moved his tongue from between my legs and caressed the soft flesh on my thighs as he continued to lap at my folds and alternate between kissing my thighs. His slow, teasing tongue allowed me to catch my breath but my tight pussy ached to feel his massive cock stretch me open inch by inch.

I cried out and he stifled my cries by covering my mouth with the large palm of his hand. I sharply exhaled through my nose as he pressed his cock up against my wetness and massaged my clit until I came again and again. Once he'd watched me leak juices out of my sopping pussy, he thrust the head of his cock an inch past my entrance. I moaned as the head of his cock with its immense girth, stretched my sensitive tightness open. He slipped inside another inch and I couldn't take it any longer. I exploded all over him, cumming and cumming over his cock as he slipped inside me one more inch. I moaned and arched my back to accommodate him as he slid inside me deeper and deeper. As his cock buried between my legs, I couldn't slow down the intensity of my climaxes. I climaxed harder and louder. Now Mace was forced to clamp his hands down around my mouth tighter so no sound could escape. He leaned over me, pressing his weight into me and brushing his lips just past my ears.

"Shhh," he whispered, "Cum quietly for daddy."

Hearing his stern, commanding voice whispering in my ear drove me crazy. I came harder than I had ever come before and squeezed my legs around him tightly, holding him firmly buried in my wetness. He continued to move his hips in a slow rhythm, making love to me and pushing me towards another intense release before I'd even recovered from the one before. With his hand pressed firmly over my mouth and his body pressed into mine, I was fully under his control. He pounded into me slower and deeper and I succumbed to every inch of pleasure he delivered. As his hand trailed from my mouth down to my throat, I found myself wanting him to squeeze it.

"Choke me… daddy…" I whimpered, thinking with my ferocious sexual appetite. I moaned as he squeezed gently around my neck. As his fingers grabbed my delicate neck, he began to pound into me harder.

"Harder…" I whimpered.

He tightened his grip just enough that I felt restrained without the danger of it and he began to thrust into me harder… and harder…

I couldn't take it. As he choked me, I came hard onto his cock, juices squirting from my wetness all over the blankets and canvas of the tent. My warm juices stuck our thighs together and as he pounded me, the loud smacking sound and grunting played erotic music throughout our campground. I dug my nails into his back and his hands squeezed me tighter and he plunged into me again and again until I came. As I came again, and my wetness tightened around his cock like a vice, he couldn't help but arrive at his own climax.

He growled with a low primal pleasure and then he grunted as he released his seed deep inside of me. Warm bursts of his seed spread inside the walls of my wetness and then all over my thighs, mixing with the juices that I'd squirted before. The deliciously nasty wetness between our thighs, drew us to remain in each other's arms, soaking up the essence of our love making until our heart rates settled and the warmth of the tent was banished due to the external cold.

Mace rolled off of me and kissed me on the cheek.

"I'm not finished with you," he whispered.

"What do you have planned?"

"My shift is another ten hours. I'd say I can give you enough orgasms to knock you out before morning."

"You aren't afraid of anything, are you?" I asked him, tracing the outline of his muscles with my fingers.

"There's nothing to be afraid of when you've got a beautiful woman to keep you occupied," he murmured.

It was a small comfort, but a comfort all the same. He ran his hands through my hair and pulled me close for another kiss. We lay there for another fifteen minutes or so and then I could feel Mace getting restless. His thigh bounced and moved around the bottom of the tent. I snaked my hands through the blanket and touched his dick. He was stiff already. I reached my hand around the base of his dick and began to stroke him to attention. He shifted his back and pushed the blankets off his torso. I raised my body from the tent and pressed my hands to his chest as I straddled Mace's torso. I pressed his hard cock against my entrance and he grasped my hips, guiding me to sit on his thick, erect cock. As his engorged cock head slipped past my entrance, I moaned and threw my head back so my hair tickled my lower back. I lowered myself another inch onto his cock and cried out again. I dug my nails into his chest and swiveled my hips as I impaled myself on his remaining length.

I moaned as I took all of him inside me. The tip of his cock was so deep between my legs that I felt a fullness in my stomach. He cried out as I bounced on it for the first time and felt him splitting me open and stimulating the deepest parts of my wetness with his hardness.

I moved my hips, bouncing them up and down as his cock stiffened between my legs.

"Ride it girl, ride it," he grunted.

My nails dug deeper into his pecs and he squeezed my hips tighter as I moved my hips faster and took his hardness deeper between my legs. I rode him slow, enjoying every inch as it slid between my legs. He groaned as I twerked my ass on his dick and rode him with a heart full of lust and passion. I grazed my nails lightly down his abs as I bounced on his cock and watching him respond to my nails on his chest made me cum long and hard. I moaned and he pressed his cock deep inside me from below. As I came he pressed his cock into me from below. He grunted and pushed his cock into me one last time before he erupted and exploded between my legs. As he came, his seed spilled from my wetness all over our thighs. His muscles shuddered and flexed as he came, revealing how defined his muscles were.

I climbed off his dick but before I could get too far, he pulled my body close to his and he climbed between my legs. He wasted no time in entering me that time. We made love for hours in every position we could think of. Towards the end of his shift, Mace pulled away from me and we departed from each other's arms with wistful passionate kisses as Mace returned to his post outside my tent. The tent still smelled like him. I caught a few valuable hours of sleep, surrounded by his scent and a warmth between my thighs that even the island's vicious cold couldn't banish.

In the morning, Tyrese's voice barked loud across the campground.

"MORNING DRILLS! MORNING DRILLS FELLAS! WE'VE BEEN SITTING ON OUR ASSES LONG ENOUGH! COME ON!"

The melody of unzipping tents and grumbles of the awakened men sounded through the camp.

Mumbles of "good morning Captain" resonated. I sat up in my tent and wrapped my blanket around my shoulders. Mace's scent had nearly faded, but in the morning cold, the last thing I wanted was to lose his comforting scent.

Outside the tent, Tyrese barked again, "Where the hell is Chubb?"

"No clue, sir," Mace replied.

"Weren't you guarding Miss Usmanov all night?"

"Yes sir, I was. But I ain't seen Chubb."

"Zhang? Is he in your tent?"

"No sir," Tim Zhang replied.

Ellis suggested, "Maybe he wandered off to take a dump."

Peña chuckled.

"Is this a laughing matter to you?" Tyrese growled.

"No, sir!"

"CHUBB!" Tyrese called, "CHUUUUBBBBBB!"

Every living creature within a twenty mile radius could have heard him. But Chester Chubb didn't. Tyrese's calls were punctuated my marked silence.

"Captain, we ought to set out and look for him," Mace suggested.

"I agree, Mister Harwood. How he could have managed to slip past you, I find most confusing."

"I spent part of the night inside Miss Usmanov's tent sir," he said to Tyrese.

"Oh?"

Heat rushed to my face as I thought Mace was about to confess.

"She was scared of the wolves sir, and I sat with her until she calmed down."

I exhaled a sigh of relief.

"We'd better set out to look for him then. Get her out of there. We need all the eyes we've got."

"Yes, sir!" The men replied in unison.

Tim Zhang got me out of my tent and they waited for me to get dressed before Tyrese split us off in groups to search for Chester. Tyrese went with me, Mace and Robbie Peña. Zhang and Ellis went off to search the western part of the island. The silence amongst the men as we searched indicated that they feared the worst had happened to him.

"BOSS!" Peña called as he searched his square footage on the patch of forest we'd made it to over a mile and a half away from camp.

"Look."

Tyrese called for Mace and my attention. I gasped when I saw it. Chester Chubb's body lay in the snow. He was undressed and splayed apart like a starfish. His head had been removed from his body and the bloody stump of his neck had drained liters of blood into the snow which soaked around the body and traced the outline of his flesh.

"God help us…" Tyrese muttered.

He commanded, "Search the perimeter for the head. It can't be far."

"Think an animal got to him, Cap'n?" Peña asked.

Tyrese never responded. It hadn't taken him long to locate Chester's head. It was suspended from a pine tree, a few feet away from his body. His face was battered and his eyes gouged out. Carved into his pale cheek was a word that I didn't recognize.

"SCHULD," Tyrese read out loud.

The three soldiers were puzzled by the discovery until Robbie chimed in.

Peña muttered, "It means debt. In German."

Part III

MACE

I'd buried so many friends before that standing next to Chester's decapitated body and his severed head swinging in the breeze like some kind of cruel warning barely hit me. I was numb. I'd been numb since the barracks on the Gulf when a bomb went off and killed all the motherfuckers sleeping except me. I'd asked "Why me?"

I'd asked "Why us?" I had asked those existential questions hundreds of thousands of times and every time I searched for an answer, the only one I got was, "Because fuck you, that's why."

Life is some cruel joke and without liquor or without women, I doubted I would make it that far. I still leaned on the liquor, but now, I had one woman on my mind — Aminata. And I couldn't believe this crime had nothing to do with her. Not like she did it. That was impossible. I'd been with her the entire night. But given the suspicions we all had regarding the crash, I figured it might do me good to keep on my toes.

Robbie carried Chubb's head back while Tyrese and I wrapped his body in a blanket and slung his giant frame between the two of us for our walk back to camp. Aminata lead the way, staying out of view of the dead body. I don't think she'd ever seen one before 'cause she was visibly shaken and even more so at the numb, silent responses of the rest of us.

We were soldiers. She was a civilian. That gulf between our lives would be impossible to bridge. The only time I came close was in the dead of night, when she saw me for who I really was without the camo, without the weapons and without a lick of clothing or pretense on my back. Even if she'd seen me at my most vulnerable, I could tell my lack of a response drove her crazy. She wanted us to pull our hair out, or do something I supposed besides acting like it was business as usual.

It wasn't business as usual however. I knew Tyrese well enough to know that he wouldn't let this slide. The German word carved into the side of our teammate's face gave us enough of a clue of what or who we were dealing with. We'd be questioned, surely. And we had to rule out an animal attack which judging by the mutilation, I thought was a pretty safe bet. Just yesterday I'd hit that mouthy bastard in the face. I shook off the feeling that maybe that fight would get me into hot water. I hadn't done anything, so I had nothing to worry about. See I knew that. But could I get the rest of the fellas to believe it?

We covered Chubb's body, resting his head alongside his torso and covering them both with a white sheet.

"Keep that fire goin'," Tyrese mumbled.

It had been the first word he'd spoken since our grim discovery. He guided Aminata to one of the large logs around the fire and sat with her, talking to her under his breath. I tried to make out what he was saying or at least read his lips, but I had nothing. Wasn't long before the other two came back. They saw the white sheet and both their faces went red. There's no mistaking what the white sheet meant.

"Was it an animal?" Ellis asked.

"No," Tyrese replied.

"May we have a look?" Ellis asked.

Tyrese nodded. Zhang approached Chester's body and pulled the sheet back gently.

"Motherfucker," Ellis remarked, making the sign of the cross dramatically, even if he was a protestant.

Ellis sat on the log next to Aminata, but he didn't acknowledge her. He buried his head in his hands and murmured what I could only assume was a prayer.

"Where's you find him?" Tim asked.

"'Bout a mile up that way," I replied.

"We aren't alone on this island," Tim replied, definitively.

"We have no evidence of that," Tyrese shot back.

"It wasn't one of us who did it!" Ellis snapped.

"Quiet, Ellis," Tyrese growled, "We have no proof of that, just like we have no proof that there's anyone else on this island. I'll be conducting an investigation as to what happened to Mr. Chubb but right now we have a pressing matter and we need to get it done before nightfall."

"We can't bury him near the tents," Robbie reminded us.

"The beach. The sand will be softer there and with all of you working, it shouldn't take too long."

"Yes, sir," we replied in unison.

Zhang nodded to me and I returned his nod. We slung Chubb's body over our shoulders and Robbie resumed the gruesome task of carrying our teammate's head.

"I'd like to pray over him if y'all don't mind," Ellis asked.

I'd only known Ellis to pray away the child support requests, but I had no problem with the man expressing his beliefs at our friend's graveside. Tyrese agreed that there shouldn't be a problem and he left us to wander down the beach as he remained at camp with Aminata.

I hated leaving her alone after what she'd seen but I had no choice. The four of us carried Chubb down to the beach and as I wrapped him up in a shroud, Peña and Ellis got started digging the hole with Zhang overseeing us and getting all specific about the depth to avoid animals desecrating the body. The irony of worrying about corpse desecration wasn't lost on any of us.

We got Chester down in the hole and then Ellis said a few prayers and then read a psalm from his worn, pocket Bible. I wanted to feel sad as I watched Zhang and Robbie cover him in sand, but a mixture of the cold and the rage blinded me to feelings of sadness. Chubb had been massacred in the middle of the night and chopped up like a pig. And whoever had done it hadn't had the decency to take on all of us at once.

"We gotta remember fellas, we're a brotherhood," Ellis said at the end of his best attempt at a sermon.

"Amen," Robbie replied, kissing the rosary that hung around his neck and tucking it back inside his shirt.

We walked back to camp. Tyrese sat outside Aminata's tent, sharpening his hunting knife.

"I need to talk to you boys one at a time. Timmy, why don't you and I go first."

They took a walk in the woods together and when they came back, Captain Lorde took a walk with Robbie, then Ellis, and then me. The three men stayed to watch Aminata and we began to walk in the opposite direction of where he'd found Chester.

"Harwood, I need you to be straight with me."

"Yes, sir."

"Did you kill Chester?"

"No, sir."

"Are you sure?"

"Yes, sir."

"Harwood, yesterday you and Chubb got into a fight. Do you care to share the details of that fight."

"No, sir," I replied. I'd been too cheeky. Tyrese stopped walking and I halted, facing him.

"Let me be clear, Harwood. I'm not giving you a choice here. I'm asking you and I expect a response. Expand on the details of that fight."

"Yes, sir."

"Good," Tyrese huffed.

"Sir, Chubb and I got into a disagreement of a racial sort."

Tyrese raised an eyebrow.

"Racial?"

Right. We were the same race, so I could see why Tyrese gave me a funny look.

"He was using derogatory words, sir."

"Mace, I know Peña's shorter than the rest of you, but I think he can handle it himself when Chester or Bubba calls someone a beaner."

"It wasn't against Robbie sir, but Aminata."

Tyrese folded his arms.

"He said what?"

"He called her the n-word, sir."

"Thank you for being honest with me, Harwood."

"Yes, sir."

I gathered that he'd heard the story from the rest of the fellas before he talked to me. The thought didn't comfort me. Despite what he'd heard, Tyrese was still looking at me with suspicion.

"I took a look at Mr. Chubb. I determined that the time he died must have been on your watch. Do you see how this looks, Harwood?"

"No, sir. I explained already that I was on watch, but I spent some time with Aminata."

"Yes, but surely you would have heard a tent unzipping —"

My mind wandered to Aminata's face, and cupping the small of her back in my arms.

"— Or heard footsteps in the snow—"

She'd lowered that beautiful tight pussy onto my cock…

"— Or maybe even noticed that anything was out of the ordinary once you left her tent."

I was quiet for too long.

"Harwood, are you listening to me?"

"Yes, sir."

"If you heard or saw anything, maybe I'd ease up on you. I understand you men have a code of honor with your captain and a code of honor with each other but I need you to level with me Harwood. We go way back. We served together. I want to know the truth. Tell the truth now, and I'll make things easier when we get back to American soil."

"I have a confession to make, sir."

Tyrese's face fell.

"You did it?"

"No, sir. I have a confession about the real reason I was distracted on my watch."

"Jesus Christ, Harwood…"

"Sir. It was Aminata. I was with her. But I wasn't there to keep her safe from wolves."

The realization hit Tyrese like a brick to the face.

"Jesus Christ, Harwood…"

He had the same reaction when he thought I'd killed a man. Ouch.

"You were…" he continued, in utter disbelief.

"Sir, one thing led to another and Miss Usmanov and I… It just sort of happened."

Tyrese clenched his fists and stopped walking. He was nothing short of apoplectic.

"Just happened?!" He growled.

"Yes, sir."

"I almost wish your sorry ass killed Chubb."

"Sir!" I protested.

"This is far worse than I could have expected, Harwood. What on earth were you thinking?!"

"Sir, she's a beautiful woman and I'm a man stranded on an isolated island."

"Then stare at Ellis getting undressed like Robbie does!"

"Sir—"

He didn't allow me a moment to respond.

"I can't believe of all the men on this team, you're the one who would be so stupid as to hop into bed with the daughter of a Russian mobster. If we get off this sorry ass island alive and her father finds out, what would you do then?"

"Sir—"

"Don't sir me! I'm not finished," Tyrese snarled, continuing his tirade.

"You don't think for a second, do you Harwood? Miss Usmanov is off-limits in every sense of the word. She is not a dangerous woman but dangerous things happen around her. Do you understand me?"

"Yes, sir."

"If I talk to Miss Usmanov, will she confirm what you've told me."

"Yes, sir. But I'll imagine she'll be pretty pissed off about it."

"No, Harwood. I'm pissed off about it."

Tyrese muttered, "Shit!"

"Sir, this still leaves the matter of who did this."

"Whoever did it must already know that you would have been distracted by Miss Usmanov. Do all of the men know?"

"No, sir. None of them do. I kept that to myself."

"The way you fellas brag, I doubt that."

"Sir, I'm telling the truth."

Tyrese shrugged.

"You haven't lied to me yet, so I got no choice but to believe you."

"How did the others do in questioning?" I asked him, hoping to figure out for myself whether any of the men on our team had murdered a fellow soldier so coldly.

"They all claimed to be asleep. Maybe Zhang's right. Maybe there's someone else on this island."

"Who would it be?"

Tyrese stroked the patchy, uneven stubble that had grown in over the past few days stranded on the island.

"Whoever it was is working for the Germans. The *Skorpione.*"

"Gang?"

"Yup, an old German biker gang that's well known in the international community."

"I think I've heard the name," I mused, uncertain if I had or hadn't.

"The beheadings are their signature. During my less-than-perfect teenage years, I had an encounter with them. They always behead their kills and they always leave a message as to why they did it. *Schuld.* It means debt.""

"Pretty gruesome way to go, if you ask me, Captain."

"It is. But I have a hard time believing that any of America's finest soldiers could be involved with people like that."

"Well then, Zhang has a point. And we aren't alone."

"Sir, I'll keep my eye out."

"Good. You do that. But Harwood, you stay away from Aminata. Don't you touch her again. I can't afford to remove you from guarding her alone, but I need you to stay alert. Women mess with that. You know it."

"Yes, sir."

"Talk to her. Let her down easy. We don't want her going to her father with any stories. Do you understand?"

"Yes, sir."

"Good. Now let's walk back. And I don't have to tell you not to share what we spoke about with the other men."

"I'll keep quiet, sir."

"Good. We don't have too much longer on this island, Mace, but we've got to make it. All of us."

"Yes, sir."

When we arrived back at camp, Tyrese ordered me and Bubba to go out on the hunt together. Bubba was a funny guy who I didn't spend much time with one on one. Out of all the men, we might have had the most similar background. I think that's why we kept to ourselves. When you grow up dirt poor, and you come to the navy for saving, then you probably don't want to talk too much about what happened before.

Plus, we'd both seen too much action to want to trade stories. There are only so many times you want to relive your friends' death. Even the funny stories become tainted by thinking about who died, who ended up different after torture in an Afghan prison, and who ended up putting a bullet in their brain all by themselves. We saw things that the world wouldn't believe we saw.

"Drink?" Ellis offered me.

That was good. No emoting and trying to get to know each other better. I hated that shit. Robbie would try it sometimes but it was much better for men to trade drink than stories. Ellis didn't make any hints that he thought I'd been involved with Chubb's death. We didn't talk at all. We got drunk and likely on account of our drunkenness, our kill was smaller than we'd wanted. Three rabbits would have been plenty, I guessed, especially considering our smaller party.

Tim had been fermenting some greens in some kind of hill-billy kimchi and we had those vegetables with the cooked rabbit meet and then Tyrese assigned me first watch. He'd done it on purpose to give me time to break things off with Aminata while the men were freshly asleep and unlikely to wake up if she took it badly. Tyrese trusted me to keep my hands off her. But I didn't know if I trusted myself.

When the fire dimmed to a glowing hot orange, the men retired to their tents, all drunker than we had been in days, except for Tyrese, who I didn't think could let his guard down that much. I entered Aminata's tent as he retired and he nodded reassuringly. He had a point. This was the right thing. This was the *only* thing. We'd have to break it off eventually anyway. She was some rich bastard's daughter and while I didn't mind the beautiful daughters of rich bastards, Oleg happened to be armed to the teeth and connected with killers far worse than whoever had gotten after Chubb. I buried the pain I felt when thinking about him. How many closer buddies had I lost to Chester? This one… I could stomach.

Aminata stared at me with her wide, knowing brown eyes as I zipped the tent shut behind me.

"You had to tell him, didn't you," she whispered.

I nodded.

"He wants you to stay away from me?"

"Yes."

"He can't make you do that!"

"Amy—"

"I don't want you to argue with me. I've already lost enough control over my life as it is."

"It doesn't have to be like this forever."

"What if we never get off this island. Then what?"

"Help is on the way. It's days away, yes, but we know that people are coming."

"What if they don't make it in time? If someone can kill Officer Chubb, what happens when they decide to come after me."

"There's no saying they're after you," I reassured her. I knew my reassurance was weak. She'd seen what happened to Chester. Aminata wasn't a soldier. Those sorts of events hit her harder than they did the rest of us. I could understand why she wanted to be held.

"My father was right," she whispered, "But he should have never sent me away."

"Your father hired me to look after you. Bet your ass I'll do my job."

I slid my knees across the tent until we were inches away from each other.

"Do you trust me, Amy?"

"Yes."

"Then trust me when I say that I'll protect you."

"I want more than that."

I leaned down and kissed her.

"So do I," I responded.

I rested my hand against her hip and she wrapped her arms around my neck. How she managed to smell like roses despite days in the woods never ceased to amaze me. I pressed my nose into her neck and she leaned over and whispered, "Do you think they're all asleep."

"Yes. They've had enough liquor to kill a rhino."

"Then you won't object to us doing this one last time."

Her hand snaked down to my manhood, throbbing through my uniform.

"I promised the Captain I'd keep my hands off of you."

"I won't kiss and tell."

"Amy…"

"One last time," she whispered, kissing my neck.

She kissed my lips and said it again, "One last time, please Mace."

How could I resist her? I didn't know a single man strong enough to resist a curvy minx like Amy. I kissed her on the lips and lowered her onto her back. I started to work my tongue on her breasts first, taking my time in the slow, erotic ritual I'd established. Each time, she responded differently. Tonight, she was no longer shy and reluctant with her top off but eager and hasty.

Nothing like forbidden fruit to drive a woman truly mad. Her breasts bounced in front of me about the size of ripe mangos. She loved when I flicked my tongue around her large Oreo-sized nipple. As I teased around the perimeter, Amy kicked her legs out and then wrapped her thighs around my torso, squeezing gently. I was never hotter than when she had me between her legs and alternated between girlish giggling and soft, gentle moans. I had her hooked and I knew it. I could pull my tongue away for a moment and she gazed up at me with soft pleading eyes.

"You're mine…" I whispered into her ear, "I don't care what Tyrese says…"

One last time, she said? I could do that. And this time I'd remind her that every inch of that tight, dark-skinned body of hers belonged to me and my big white cock.

"More…" she whimpered as my tongue trailed down to her stomach.

I moved back up to her nipples, rewarding her for her patience and she moaned and then whimpered, "I'm cumming…" after a few more moments of stimulation. She ran her hands through my hair, digging into my scalp and bucking her hips up responsively as nipple stimulation alone pushed her to the edge of an intense climax. She settled into the sheets, a smile creeping across her face.

"That's never happened to me before."

"Really?"

She nodded shyly.

"Would you like for it to happen again?"

She nodded and I went to work on her nipples, changing my swift circles to gentle flicking across her nipples and then sucking on them hard. She came quickly and her thighs grew damp with her juices as her mound emanated heat. I couldn't keep my lips away from her pussy any longer. I spread her legs wide and planted a few quick kisses on her tummy before I opened her thighs apart like a hot sticky bread roll. Her buttery juices dribbled down her thick brown thighs.

I kissed her inner thighs and she trembled from the ticklish sensation on her legs. I kissed her other thigh and then thrust my tongue and lips all over the spots where her juices spilled so I could lap up every last drop of her juices as they leaked out of her sopping heat.

She moaned as I used a finger to work between her legs. I stuck my finger into her honeypot and more juices gushed out as I pressed it in deep and rubbed the pad of my finger up against her g-spot. She squeezed her thighs shut and I muscled them open.

"Keep your legs open," I demanded.

She spread them wider, eager to please me, eager to spread that tasty little pussy out for daddy to eat. I licked my lips and lowered them between her legs while one of my fingers stimulated her engorged g-spot. I wrapped my lips around her clit and added another finger between her legs as I lapped at her pussy lips. With her lips dripping wet and my tongue sliding between them, I contrasted it with the thrusting of my hard fingers, sliding along the curves of her pussy walls in the most pleasurable rhythm. She bucked her hips upward, fucking my fingers with her tightness as my tongue swirled around her clit.

She moaned as her hips responded to my devout pleasuring. She grabbed the sheets and cried out, moaning carelessly as she came all over me. She grew wetter as she came and her hot juices spilled onto my face and over my hands as she leaked honey-sweet juices from her divine tightness. Holding back when I had such a deliciously sweet pussy spread before me would have been impossible. I pulled my fingers out of her wetness and she whimpered as I left her tight hole vacant.

Aminata was a shuddering, whimpering mess desperate to be filled. In the heat of the moment, I no longer cared about waking up Tyrese, or about whatever fate would await me if I was caught breaking my word to my captain and enjoying the fresh hot pussy that Aminata had served up to me. I was only a man after all, and stranded on an island with only other men it was my instinct to claim the juiciest pussy in sight and make her mine. I stripped my shirt off and she clawed for my abs as they were exposed in the tent.

Every inch of my body was utterly fascinating to her and I indulged her curiosity. As her nails ran down my rippling abs, I worked my pants off. She tugged on my dog tags, pulling me to her lips and kissing me hard.

"This won't be the last time," she whispered.

Before I could protest, she drove me closer again with her heels. I pressed the weight of my body into hers, feeling how delicate she lay on the floor and how euphoric it was to have her ready and waiting, horny and eager for me to slide between her legs. But her proclamation of this not being the last time? I couldn't be so sure about that. Eventually, I'd have to put my orders first. But not yet.

I pressed the head of my cock up against her entrance. She squirmed with delight and anticipation that had gone on far too long for her liking.

I teased her by sliding in just the head and withdrawing it quickly. She gasped and then pouted.

"You're such a tease…"

"You need someone to make the rules."

She couldn't argue with that so she spread her legs wider, hoping this time I wouldn't taunt her.

I slid in another two inches and then pulled my cock out to meet her desperate, wild-eyed expression.

"Please, Mace…"

I taunted her once more, sliding in only a few inches which was enough to make her let out a soft moan but not enough to satisfy the aching emptiness between the spongy walls of her tight little pussy. I grabbed her hips, and as her soft flesh spilled between my fingers, I slid my rigid tool deep inside her wetness. Her well-stimulated pussy was hot and gripped my cock tightly as I buried it inside her. She moaned and her soft spongy entrance clung to my tumescent member.

"Ohhhhh."

Her moans egged me on, forced me to go further than I wanted to. If I could only have her once tonight… that would be enough. That could be enough to keep me for the next few days at least. As the tip of my cock brushed the deepest walls of her pussy, I knew I couldn't stand using her tight little hole only once for the night. I leaned over to kiss her as I drove my cock into her tightness with deep, forceful thrusts. She grabbed onto my cheeks as I kissed her and she moaned into my mouth as I pummeled her tightness. As I drove my cock into her faster, her pussy was hotter and hotter and her flesh burned beneath my touch like a furnace.

She exploded when she came for the first time and her juices soaked my thighs, filling the tent with the soft scent of her love honey. Her juices around my cock and the tightness of her heat drove me over the edge and I could barely hold back as the cum nearly erupted out of my cock. I pulled out of her and then flipped her onto her stomach, pressing her into the floor of the tent. Something primal came over me as I pressed my weight into her, coated with her juices and with the mixture of our scents. I had a desperate urge to cum inside her pussy and I had to have it now.

She was mine… In a camp with six other men, I had been the first to claim her pussy and I was the only man who could have her, bent over in her tent, presenting that precious tight little hole for daddy's taking. I spread her ass cheeks apart and jammed a thumb between them. She moaned, but didn't complain about the pain, only jiggling her ass cheeks around them.

"This is *my* pussy," I growled as I slammed the full length of my cock into her pussy from behind.

She cried out loud.

"Ow…"

"Tell me whose pussy this is…" I growled, grabbing onto a tuft of her hair and holding it tightly.

She trembled slightly, but she didn't falter, she didn't break her ultimate submission to me. Bent over on all fours, she replied with a desperate whimper, "It's your pussy, daddy…"

"Good. And while we're apart… you're not to let anyone else between those thighs of yours…"

"Yes, daddy…" she moaned.

"Good. Now daddy's going to put his cock deep inside your pussy…"

"Yes…" she moaned.

I slammed my cock into her again, pounding between her legs harder and harder until she came. As she came, she collapsed into the tent and I pressed my weight on top of her as I rammed into her pussy from behind. Her soft ass cheeks bounced against my torso and I released my tight grip on her hair, moving my hand around to her mouth and then down to her pretty, swan-like neck.

I hesitated before applying pressure on her neck. I wanted to own her in every sense of the word but I'd already pushed it… Then that naughty woman wrapped up in the disguise of a good girl whimpered the three words every guy wants to hear.

"Choke me daddy," she moaned.

I wrapped my hands around her neck, gently enough to block some air but not enough to hurt her. I squeezed…

"Harder…" she whimpered.

I pounded into her tight pussy from behind as I choked her with my strong hands. Within seconds she exploded all over me, more wetness gushing from her tight hole than I'd ever seen before. She was squirting and juices splashed from her pussy all over my cock and in a massive wet spot on the sheets beneath us.

"Cum… inside… me…" she whimpered.

I changed my mind. Those were the only three words any guy wants to hear. I pulled my cock out of her and then adjusted her position so she could steady her own weight again. As she arched her back so her ass would make the perfect heart shaped position, I smacked the voluptuous brown cheeks. She moaned as I slid inch by inch between her legs again. Her tightness dripped juices from the moment the head of my cock pumped between her exposed lips. I groaned as I thrust inside her, enjoying every inch of her wrapped around my cock. I thrust between her legs gently at first but then my gentle lovemaking transformed into quick pounding. I kept my strokes fast and deep at first but then as I plunged deeper between her sticky walls, I began to make love to her more slowly.

"Yes… Cum inside me…" she moaned.

I thrust again, driving between her legs harder… and harder…

"Cum inside me, Mace…"

Hearing her moan that over and over again drove me wild. I grunted as I spilled my seed between her thighs.

Yeah, she was right. This wouldn't be the last time.

AMINATA (AMY)

Mace snuck out in the middle of the night. I had fallen asleep in his arms and for a few moments, I'd betrayed myself by thinking that it could last forever. I smelled the sheet where he'd been and wrapped myself up in his scent for a few moments longer. I couldn't stand not having him by my side. After what had happened to the other man, I didn't feel safe. How could Papa have thought this was a better option than staying by his side?

I heard the men getting up in the morning and heard the sound of their morning drills — an aggressive cacophony of pants, growls and other grotesque noises men make when they exert themselves too hard. On top of that, Tyrese's barking commands never ceased. Once the men were done, Tyrese made them all get breakfast. We had all made it through another night. Tyrese informed the men of a communication he'd received from the beach. There was occasional communication with our would be rescuers, except Tyrese learned that they had been delayed another day. I huddled deeper beneath the covers as I heard the news. Another day in danger. Another day in the untamed wilderness.

Tyrese sent all the men off into the woods to investigate. Afterward, he called my name.

"Miss Usmanov! Good morning!"

I guess I didn't have the option to sleep in either.

"Good morning," I called back, hoping he would hear my tired tone and let me be.

"I'd like to talk with you outside the tent now if that's alright."

"Yes…sir…"

"Oh ma'am, I appreciate the respect but there's no need to call me sir."

I bundled up as much as I could before joining Tyrese outside. The fire roared almost as tall as he was and he sat on the log before it.

"Come warm up and get some breakfast. You must be cold."

I nodded and sat next to him as he spooned some leftover meat and powdered eggs into a tin bowl for me. I ate ravenously and then to Tyrese's surprise, asked for vodka to help wash the rest of it down.

"Satisfied?"

"Yes."

"Good. Now Miss Usmanov, I believe I owe you a security briefing but due to the sensitive nature of all this, I wanted us to do this alone."

"I understand."

"Your father is a very powerful man, Miss Usmanov, and I'm gathering that you are only now beginning to understand the full depths of his power."

"My father is a diplomat. That's all I know."

"He's done a good job raising you, Miss Usmanov."

"Thank you."

Tyrese settled into more unpleasant business.

"After much discussion, and partly due to my radio call

yesterday, I believe we have a suspect in Officer Chubb's killing."

"You know who did it?"

"Not exactly. But we at least know the killer's motive."

I listened intently. Tyrese ran his hands over his bald, shiny head. He reminded me of what my father might have looked like if he hadn't died when I was an infant. Tyrese never faltered, never showed any fear despite the powerlessness of our situation. He made a good leader.

"The word carved into Officer Chubb's face gave us a clue. We have good reason to believe that a German biker gang is responsible for the killing."

"So it is someone on our team working for them?"

"I don't know. With the storm coming in, communication wasn't the best."

"We can rest assured that whoever this is might strike again. And that's what we're waiting for."

"For them to kill?!"

"You will be safe, Miss Usmanov. I promise. But we won't be able to find out more about this killer until they make another attempt on one of my men."

"That's savage!"

"My men are born survivors. If they can't handle a German, they can't handle anything."

"And you're sure it's a German? What do the Germans have against my father?"

I'd met plenty of Germans in my life, both at boarding school in Switzerland, and during our vacations to Berlin and Croatia. Papa had never given any indication that there were problems between them.

"As I understand it, the rift between your brothers has created some challenges and as a result, one of your brothers has offended the big boss of some German biker gang."

My heart sank.

"It's me they're after then. I'm the reason people are going to die."

Tyrese gave me his best stern, fatherly voice.

"Listen Miss Usmanov. You aren't responsible for the actions of those men. Your father chose a specific life and he gave you an option not to be involved in it. Just stay safe. That's all your father wants for you."

"If someone's trying to kill me, then none of us are safe."

"For now, we're pretty convinced that they're only trying to send a message.

"Excuse me if I can't buy that…"

"You don't have to. Keep your wits about you. That's all you really need. And if you have any questions, I want you to come talk to me. Don't speak with any of the others."

I nodded.

"Not even Mace," he added.

I lowered my head into the flask of vodka.

"Yes, sir."

"Miss Usmanov, I don't mean to involve myself in your personal affairs but currently, I have forbidden Mace Harwood from engaging with you and I want to explain to you that I am aware of what has been happening and I don't want it to happen again. Is that clear?"

"Yes, sir."

"Officer Harwood is putting himself in a difficult situation with you. And both of us know that the world Officer Harwood inhabits is very different from the one that you do."

"Yes, sir."

"He's a drunk. He's unruly. He's an absolute loud-mouth. You need to be careful with him. He's not suited to someone like you. Miss Usmanov, you are royalty. Your father is royalty. I have a lot of respect for that."

"Yes, sir," I replied, thoroughly shamed by his forwardness in breaching the problem of me and Mace.

After my talk with Tyrese, he changed the subject to more pleasantries until the men returned from their assignments, all of them dripping in sweat. Bubba Ellis and Robbie had some blood smeared on their clothes and skin from cleaning animals they'd set traps for the night before.

"You two stink. Couldn't you have at least sponged off before coming back here?" Tyrese commented.

Ellis shot Robbie a glare.

"Penny can't keep his eyes to hisself so I won't be taking my clothes off near him," Bubba blurted out.

"Sir!" Robbie protested.

"Watch your mouth, Ellis," Tyrese warned.

"What? It ain't a secret. We can all hear him beating his meat and moaning in the tent. Ain't no women 'round here. Ain't no porn. We all know what he's thinking and it's time somebody said it."

"That's *enough,* Ellis."

"Yes, sir," Bubba replied with a surly tone.

"Peña you step out into the woods and clean yourself. Ellis, get to splitting logs with Harwood and Zhang. When he comes back you'll take a turn. And Ellis? Stop being such a goddamned baby."

Robbie sulked off into the woods and Ellis joined Mace and Tim Zhang with the food. I hadn't so much as looked at Mace. Especially after my talk with Tyrese, I didn't want to rouse his suspicions. Mace was doing a good job of avoiding me too.

"Captain Lorde?" I called after a few minutes of stabbing sticks into the snow. The boredom was getting to me.

"What is it, Miss Usmanov?"

"I need to go for a walk."

"Fine. I'll have Tim Zhang escort you."

"I don't need an escort."

"Miss Usmanov, need I remind you that a man was killed in these woods?"

"I promise I won't go far. Ellis should be on the path, sir. I'll call out for help if I need any."

"It's broad daylight, Captain," Tim added in my defense, flashing me a friendly wink.

"Fine. But be back in five minutes."

"I will, sir."

"Take this."

Tyrese handed me a large hunting knife.

"Sir?"

"I'm sure you won't need to use it. But in a pinch…"

"Thanks."

I gripped the knife handle and walked down the path away from camp. I crunched through the snow, following the line of trees and the bootprints of the other men. After relieving myself a few feet off of the main path, I heard whistling in the woods. The path to the spring was along the route I'd been walking. The whistling, which I assumed was Ellis came from about a hundred feet off. I stepped behind a large pine tree as the whistling grew louder, but not closer.

I followed the sound at first, and then I found bootprints which veered off the main path. Ellis' suspicions about Robbie's sexuality had nothing to do with why he veered off the path. He was up to something. Tyrese had warned me not to get too far and I had a time limit. I slipped between the trees, trying to kick the snow around my shoe prints to disguise my tracks as I approached.

Ellis was whistling what sounded like some kind of Civil War era folk music. He started to sing out loud and I clapped my hands to my mouth to avoid laughing. He sounded like a drunk Johnny Cash. But less good — obviously. I snuck closer and when I caught my first glimpse of him, I hid behind the largest tree I could find. As I exhaled, I tried to get my breath quieter and quieter. I thought I was safe and out of sight until Ellis stopped whistling.

"Who's there?" He called.

"Robbie?"

I held my breath and Ellis resumed whistling. I waited for the longest three minutes of my life before I peeked my head around the corner of the tree and saw Ellis diving into a spring. Steam escaped from the surface of the water. Hot springs. The bastard had found hot springs off the beaten path and hadn't bothered to inform the rest of the men who had been washing themselves in icy waters of a stream that cut across their main hunting range.

Sneaky, sneaky.

While I had no desire to take a look at Ellis' junk, I couldn't help but catch a full view of it. Ew. He was covered in tattoos and I mean covered. In his starched military camouflage, he was the boy-next-door personified. I stared at the tattoos that flanked Ellis' rib cage and his arms. He even had tattoos on his neck that he somehow kept covered up too.

On his arm, there were words, written around a large eagle. If I could make it a little closer, maybe I could see. I'd have to wait until his back was turned. Ellis dunked his head beneath the waters of the spring and I bolted for the next largest tree I could find to hide behind. That got his attention.

"Hello?"

"If any of you motherfuckers is playing a joke on me, you'll find out you've been messing with the wrong guy!"

He bellowed and then chuckled, presumably at himself, before he continued to wash himself in the spring. I peered out from behind the tree, my breath shuddering with terror. Discovery might mean more trouble than I was willing to deal with. Ellis was distorted again and I caught the tattoo on his arm. It was in German. As I'd suspected. From my vantage point, I could catch sight of his other tattoos even better. All of them were in German…

Tyrese had warned me about the German biker gangs, and how Chester had been killed using their signature move. Ellis was hiding probably fifty tattoos, many of them written in German, or using old German symbols from World War II. I peeled myself away from what I'd seen and crouched down behind the tree trunk. I couldn't leave without alerting Ellis, so I had no choice but to wait for him to be finished cleaning himself up. I didn't have to wait long. He got out of the hot spring and after toweling himself off, he stepped into his socks and then his shoes, and then buttoned himself up to cover all his tattoos once again.

He walked right past me without even noticing, and he returned to the path back to camp, whistling to himself as he left. When I could no longer hear Ellis' whistles, I ran back towards the path, and then back towards camp. Snow had started to fall and neither of our footprints were visible in the snow. When I got back to camp, Tyrese stood at the entrance to the path with his arms folded.

"Where have you been?"

"I-I got lost," I lied.

"Miss Usmanov, with all due respect, this is exactly why I

didn't want you going out alone. I understand you're a grown woman but your father has put us in our care."

"Yes, sir. I apologize."

"Well, no harm done. But next time, I won't be sending you off alone."

There wouldn't be a next time. And we didn't have anything to fear for much longer. Ellis had done it. He'd killed Chester. He was the one working for the German gangs. I'd just have to prove it some other way besides his tattoos. I couldn't explain to Tyrese how I'd come to see them. If I explained what had happened, he might think that this was another situation like mine with Mace. He might accuse me of being a liar, or a whore. Until I had proof, there was only one person I could trust with what I'd seen. There was only one person who would listen to me.

Unfortunately, Tyrese kept his eye on both of us, and during the daytime we had no time alone. Tyrese had fished out a deck of cards and despite Ellis' loud insistence on playing poker, we settled for "Egyptian Rat Screw", a game I'd never heard of. I preferred to play either poker myself, or Russian card games, but I wouldn't find myself agreeing with Ellis after what I'd seen. We ate heartily and drank even more. That night, Tim Zhang kept first watch over me and I slept peacefully during his shift. Tyrese took over after that, and I remained in my tent until morning when he began to rouse the men.

That morning, I determined that I had to see Mace alone. Tyrese sent Peña and Zhang off to clean more meat and check traps. Ellis went off to take another walk in the woods — I can't keep track of the excuse he gave — and that left me alone with Mace and Tyrese.

"Tyrese, I'd like to take another walk."

"I can't walk with you, I've got to head down to the beach and see who I can get a hold of with this radio."

"I could walk her, Captain," Mace suggested.

Tyrese narrowed his eyes and looked from me to Mace, barely disguising his suspicions.

"Fine. I trust you, Harwood."

"Yes, sir," Mace responded respectfully.

Tyrese walked off down to the beach. Once he left, Mace approached with his arms folded.

"What are you up to?"

"I don't want to go for a walk."

"I figured. But if we want to talk… we can't do it out here."

"The men went that way," I replied, gesturing towards the path.

"We'll go another way then. You seem desperate to talk with me."

"I am."

"Bundle up then. I'm taking a shot gun."

I waited for Mace to suit up and grab a shotgun and we started down the Southern path away from the camp. Mace held the shotgun over his shoulder.

"What do you want to talk about."

"I saw something yesterday during my walk."

"Spill, Amy."

"I saw where Ellis went when he said he was headed to the stream."

"Bubba?"

"Yes."

"Okay, he lied and got a bit of quiet time. Can't say I blame him."

"I followed him."

"Amy—"

"Just listen to me, Mace."

He stopped walking and I stopped. The woods were quiet without the crunching of our boots in the snow. Under any other circumstances, the island might have been beautiful. I'd grown accustomed to the bitter chill and now, it didn't even feel so cold.

"I saw Ellis' tattoos."

"Wait he didn't have his clothes on?"

I was getting ahead of myself, losing myself in wanting to spit out what I'd seen. Of course, Mace required an explanation.

"He was at a hot spring. Right. He must have found one off the path and that's where he went."

"Hot springs? That bastard. I've been freezing my nuts off out here."

"I saw him *unclothed*."

"Under other circumstances, I'd be jealous."

"It's not funny Mace! His tattoos were in German. He's the killer. He killed Chester Chubb."

Mace frowned.

"This is a serious accusation, Amy."

"I know. I have no proof. All I have is what I've seen. Think about it Mace. You men are closer to each other than anyone in the world. Yet Ellis is funny about one particular thing, and it's what ties him to the Germans."

"What you're saying does make sense."

"What do we do?"

"We can't do anything but keep an eye on him," Mace replied matter-of-factly.

"That's it?!"

He was the one holding a shot gun. He was the one trained to raid military bases and assassinate terrorists if necessary. How could his response to a fellow SEAL killing a soldier be so measured and calm.

"What more do you want me to say, Amy?"

"Anything! You're a soldier, Mace. Isn't that what soldiers do?"

"I can't rush in places guns blazing!"

"Why not?!"

"We need more information, Amy."

"I thought you of all people would take me seriously."

"I am taking you seriously."

"Whatever."

I turned on my heels to walk away from him, but Mace grabbed my arm before I could get too far.

"Not so fast," he grumbled, pulling me back to face him.

"Let go of me, Mace."

"No."

"Let go!"

"I need you to calm down, Amy."

"I am calm!"

"No. You're not. But your safety depends on acting like you are. If Ellis is the man you think he is, then he's dangerous. You can't act differently. At all. Do you understand?"

His grip on my arm softened.

"Yes. I understand."

"Good."

"Are you going to tell Tyrese?"

"Not yet. But I'm going to make sure Ellis isn't watching your tent tonight."

"Okay."

He leaned in and kissed me. I pulled away, surprised.

"I thought we weren't going to do this anymore."

"How the hell am I supposed to keep my hands off you?"

"Self control?"

Mace grinned.

"I've never been too good at that."

He kissed me again and his hand wandered to my waist where he squeezed me and pulled me closer again.

"Mm, I've missed touching you."

"You're going to get us both into trouble if you don't stop," I murmured.

He pulled away again and pressed his forehead to mine. His nose was cold as it grazed against my cheek.

"Why should I take you back to camp when I can have my way with you out here?"

"Out here in the woods?"

"There's a nice big pine over there...I could press you up against it and warm you up real quick."

"What if Tyrese hears us?"

"The Captain will be on the beach for at least twenty more minutes."

He kissed me again before I could protest. The more he kissed me, the more he had me hooked. His lips were warm, and perfectly soft, providing necessary comfort to me in the cold. His warm hands slid beneath my fleece and his appeals to heat me up became that much more alluring.

"We have to get off the path…"

He kissed my neck and nodded before nuzzling the tip of his nose into the crook of my neck. He led me just off the path and pressed me up against a big pine tree just like he'd promised. As he kissed me, the scent of pine needles and fresh snow reminded me of the beauty of Russia in the winter. The cold and dark that repelled most foreigners would always feel like home to me. And right here, with Mace's lips pressed against mine, I felt more at home than I had since I'd left my father's side in America.

"Don't stop…" I whispered. He grabbed my buttocks and hiked me off the ground, balancing my butt between his strong palms. He carried me like I was weightless and kissed me until I thought I would burst from anticipation. We hadn't much time and the urgency made all our actions lustier and more desperate. He peeled my pants off just over my butt and his hands warmed the gooseflesh that appeared upon my butt's exposure to the cold. As I shuddered in his grasp, he whispered into my ear, "Don't worry, Amy. I promise I'll warm you up."

He pulled his pants down just over his butt and pressed his hardness against the entrance to my pussy. I moaned as he slid between my thighs, cutting through my slit like a hot knife through butter. He pumped between my legs, jamming his cock into my heat and thrusting faster and faster. I ran my hands over his neck, clutching onto him and wrapping my thighs tight around his torso as he pumped between my legs. As heat rose in my chest, the cold no longer bothered me. I couldn't hold back any longer. I exploded in pleasure, cumming hard on Mace's thick, long cock as he drove his dick deep between my legs. My juices squirted around my thighs and dampened the fabric that clung desperately to our legs as we made illicit love up against a tree. Snow started to fall and as the flakes touched Mace's back, they melted and rolled in large drops over his muscles. The snow touched my nose and tingled on the bits of my flesh where it touched. The fresh snow combined with the heat generated by our bodies intertwined together pushed me over the edge, stimulating me to cum again… and again…

"Yes, daddy…"

"Take my cock, Amy. Take daddy's big hard cock…"

His deep, masculine commands drove me over the edge again and I came furiously on his cock. As I came this time, I could sense him getting closer to a climax of his own. I dug my nails into his back and bucked my hips upward to meet the slow, deep thrusts of his big veiny dick.

"Harder…" I whimpered.

He obliged, driving into me slow and forcefully. As he withdrew his cock a few inches, I slammed my heels into his buttocks, forcing him to lodge his hardness deep inside my dripping cunt. He groaned and erupted between my legs as my surprising move forced my pussy to clench tightly around his invading cock. As he came, his juices squirted in warm, thick spurts against the walls of my pussy, heating me up from within as he hurriedly pulled his dick out of me.

We rushed to get our clothes on and to hold onto the warmth that we'd generated only a half-mile away from camp.

"We don't have long," Mace told me.

We could expect Tyrese or the other men returning to camp soon. As we walked back, Mace grew even more stern and solemn than usual. He stopped me a few feet away from camp.

"Don't do anything different. I will come up with a plan to handle Ellis and I'll make sure I get the final shift at your tent tonight."

"Okay."

"Amy… I love you, okay? I won't let anything happen to you."

"Did you just say—"

"Yes. I did."

"Are you sure?"

"What do you mean I am sure?"

"I hear how the other men think of me. Like I'm just some spoiled princess."

Mace reached for my hand and brought it to my lips.

"You followed a dangerous SEAL into the woods alone. You aren't a spoiled princess. You're brave. It ain't your fault that you lived a good life."

"I love you too, Mace."

"I know that."

"But I had to say it."

"So did I."

He kissed me. He was reluctant at first, as if saying we loved each other for the first time made this next kiss new again. He tasted my lips sensuously and then thrust his tongue into my mouth, playing with mine and allowing me to taste his warmth. When he pulled away from me, I was dripping wet again. I could feel his cum leaking against my thigh and my wetness ached to feel him there again. He could see my hunger for him written on my face. He smiled and kissed me on the forehead.

"Not yet, Miss Usmanov. Later tonight. Be patient."

For him, I could be anything. Even patient.

We were the first to return to camp. Mace stoked the fire back to life and made me a cup of instant coffee. We were running low on supplies and with the latest delay, we would run out of coffee about three days before help came. I didn't relish the thought. At least we still had liquor, which had miraculously survived the sinking boat. I guess the SEAL team really was prepared for anything.

Tyrese returned from the beach with more bad news. He hadn't been able to get in touch with anyone and he couldn't pinpoint the exact time our rescue would arrive. He had an estimate, but even I could tell he wasn't confident. Tyrese helped Mace with the fire and then they spoke for a while privately. I couldn't tell what about. The rest of the men returned after lunch. Tyrese didn't have many questions. The longer we spent on the island, the less interested he was in playing drill sergeant. The mission should have been over by now anyway.

For the first time in a while, I thought about my father and wondered if he would be forced to pay these men for all the trouble they'd gone through. My mind wandered somewhere darker afterward, as I realized that not all the men who had left America would make it home. And we may lose more yet. I couldn't help but stare at Ellis as the day wore on. My eyes followed him wherever they could. He didn't catch me looking and he was hardly aware of my suspicions of him. Bastard. How could he be so calm knowing that he killed a fellow soldier. He'd betrayed his oath, his loyalty to his country, and sold out for a pack of German thugs. How could men hide such despicable actions behind blond hair and a smile?

That evening, we ate a stew with some potatoes Ellis dug up as well as a mixture of rabbit meat and goose. Tim Zhang cooked it all up and added some of the fermented vegetables he'd been storing since our arrival. The men drank their bellies full after we finished off the pot of stew. When the men got to talking with each other, I didn't have much to say and I usually didn't listen to them. That night, I thought about my brothers. They had been through so much together and now that they were fighting, their disagreement had caused even more problems. I missed going hunting with Vasily. I missed riding through the fields behind Papa's house with Boris as he lamented his desire to run away from everything and write poetry. I even missed Feodor, with his excessive drinking and addiction to gambling.

I drowned my troubles in vodka. I drank considerably less than the men did, but I was properly woozy by the time I was ready to head to bed. Tyrese posted Robbie at my door for the first shift and the men stayed up late carousing until the end of Robbie's shift when Mace took over. They exchanged a few words and Mace thumped him on the back goodbye. He sat quietly outside of my tent until the men were asleep and then he crawled in, sidling up next to me.

"Good night, Amy," he whispered.

I sat straight up, eager to listen to Mace's plan. He pressed his forehead to mine and whispered his intentions into the dark. I listened as he explained how he would follow Ellis the next day and collect any evidence. There had to be a murder weapon somewhere and more evidence about how on earth he decapitated Chubb. I agreed that following him was a good idea and then Mace kissed me on the cheek.

"I'm drunk," he murmured.

"So am I."

"Tonight, I just want to sleep with you. Just…sleep."

"Me too."

"I'll wake up in an hour or two. Once I've slept this off."

I pulled him down into the sheets and wrapped my arms around him. He was so solid and strong. He could take care of both of us. I knew it. I didn't hear when Mace left my tent, but he must have. In the morning, I awoke to Tyrese's voice and then Mace's engaged in conversation in hushed tones.

"You didn't see anything?" Tyrese whispered.

"No, sir."

"Were you *with* her last night?"

"We spoke, sir. That was it. Nothing romantic."

"We've got to head out and look for him then."

"Before the others wake up, Captain?"

"Yes. I'll head out. You get Miss Usmanov and tell her what's happening."

Tyrese walked off and I unzipped my tent.

"Tell me what?" I asked Mace, who seemed surprised that I was awake.

"Get dressed. Come out here, then we'll talk."

I did as he asked and stood inches away from him, worried about what he was going to say.

"What's wrong?"

"Robbie is missing. He's just gone."

Part IV

MACE

We found Robbie's body about a half mile away from camp. His head hung from a tree the same way Chester's had except his eyes had been left in his head and tears of blood streamed down his face. The same word was carved in his cheeks. His body hadn't been mutilated further and we were left with the same task of burial and a funeral. This time, we needed Tyrese's help and he kept Aminata at his side the entire time. We wrapped Robbie in a white blanket and carried him down to the beach. Tyrese, Tim and Bubba dug the hole for him while I went back to camp to gather what remained of his things. A few personal affects had survived the sinking ship. A rosary. A laminated psalm translated into Spanish. A photograph of him kissing another man on the lips. I wrapped those things in his black kerchief and brought them down to the beach.

I helped the men dig the rest of the hole. Six feet deep. Bubba and Tim were both beet red by the time we finished. Tyrese was visibly upset, brooding and he eyed each of us suspiciously. I couldn't gauge Amy's reaction. During the day time and under Tyrese's watchful eye, she wasn't prone to making any moves that might expose our continued dalliances to him. We lowered Robbie's body into the grave and I dropped his personal items down over him. Tyrese shoveled the first scoop of sand onto Robbie's body and that's when it really hit me. He was dead. Decapitated. Killed and skinned like one of our geese or rabbits. When I joined the army, my ma always told me that once you can take an animal to slaughter, you can kill a man. I didn't believe her until I joined the SEALs and saw it with my own two eyes. Some men took to killing more than others. Whoever had killed Chubb and Peña took to it like a fish to water.

Once Robbie was buried and a mound of sand heaped upon his frigid final resting place, we stood around solemnly. Chubb's funeral had been one thing. But Robbie? He hadn't had problems with anyone, except Ellis recently. He was a team player. A bit of an ass, but a good man. What could any of us say to memorialize him, or to explain it. I'd listened to Amy's suspicions about Bubba, but if he had killed Robbie, he was doing a good job of concealing his feelings about the matter. He appeared more torn up than the rest of us. Captain Lorde only seemed angry.

"I'd like to say a few words," Tim chimed in, his black hair sticking to the back of his neck as he stared solemnly at Robbie's grave.

"Go ahead, Zhang."

"Robbie was a good man. We served together many times in many countries all over the world. He was a great teammate, the best gym buddy you could ask for, and he made fried rice that could put my mom's to shame. I'll miss him and I know the rest of us will to. Rest in peace, bud."

Tyrese closed his eyes and the rest of us followed suit. I thought about Robbie for a minute, and how whoever had done this to him hadn't given a second thought to who he was leaving behind at home. I opened my eyes. Tim's were still closed and so were Tyrese's. Bubba stared at me, with an intense, angry blue gaze. We broke away from the funeral and Bubba approached me, jabbing a finger into my chest.

"You were on guard last night. You let this happen."

I didn't respond to him. Bubba's veins bulged out of his forehead angrily as he waited for a response, or perhaps he'd been hoping for a confession. His blue uniform was starched and buttoned all the way up to the collar. His hands were red, as affected from the cold as mine were. His lips quivered in fury as he waited in vain.

"You ain't even gonna say anything? You were on watch last night, Harwood so I want you to tell me what happened to him."

"I didn't see anything. I swear to you, Ellis."

"Your word means nothing to me. Two of our men are dead and I've never liked your attitude, Harwood."

He was angry, and taking that anger out on me. Nothing I said would change his mind. Nothing I said could make him feel less hurt. Or perhaps, less guilty. He was the one who had fought with Robbie yesterday, calling him out for the secret truth that we had all simply ignored about Robbie. The man had family. He had kids. This was supposed to be a simple mission, over in only a few days.

And now he was gone. I'd waited too long for Bubba Ellis' liking.

He stormed away before I could give him the answers he wanted or more likely, the answer he didn't want. I knew nothing about Robbie's death except whoever had done it must have been one of us. I didn't buy this theory of a Lone Ranger striking in the middle of the night. That didn't add up. Robbie wouldn't have wandered off alone and he wouldn't have let a stranger get close enough to do this to him.

I didn't call after Bubba. Odd behavior for someone who Aminata suspected of murdering him. I knew Bubba and that anger of his was real. If he could get all worked up about that, could he really have been the one to kill Peña? Could a blunt instrument like Bubba really have a poker face that good?

Back at camp, Tyrese pulled me aside, leaving Amy sitting on the log with Bubba and Tim, who stared at the fire, both hungry but unable to eat. Robbie's loss hit all of us hard.

"We need to talk about what happened, Mace," Tyrese spoke once we were out of ear shot.

"I don't know what happened. The whole night, I was up. Listening. I swear to you, I would have heard if someone dragged Robbie off, Captain."

"We're down to three men, and myself. I know that I didn't do it, but Mace, it doesn't look good for you. Is there anything that you have to tell me?"

"No, sir."

"I want to trust you, Hardwood. But I can't trust anyone right now."

"Will you be talking to the other men, sir?"

"Of course, Mace. Of course. But only one of those men was on duty. You."

"I can assure you, Captain. I had nothing to do with Chester's death and I had nothing to do with Robbie's."

"I want to trust you, but I can't. I can't trust any of you."

"Sir, I ought to tell you something."

"Spill."

"Amy saw something during her walk in the woods the other day. She asked me to keep it private but I can't think of a better time to let you know."

"Enough with the suspense, Harwood."

"She followed Officer Ellis into the woods and saw his arms tattooed with something German. She believes there is a connection between Officer Ellis and Chester's death, sir."

"And now, Peña's."

"Yes, sir."

"Impossible."

"But, sir!"

"No," Tyrese insisted, "It's impossible."

"Is there any reason you aren't open to the possibility?"

Captain was starting to make me mad. And when I get mad, I get reckless too. Hadn't we lost enough of our men playing it safe? How could Tyrese dismiss what Aminata had found so quickly.

"I'm going to need a better explanation than that."

"Mind your rank, Harwood."

"If I may be frank, sir. We have served together for years, under Captain Scott, under Captain Gary. I know you better than any of these other men and right now, I don't give a damn about military formality."

"Military formality is the only thing keeping all of us from descending into chaos," Tyrese insisted.

His eyes were bloodshot from lack of sleep. He'd been up all night too, just like I had. And he hadn't heard anything either. Robbie's death was ripping him apart just as it ripped me apart. He knew that whoever had done this had pulled the wool over both of our eyes and he hated it. Believing that I was the killer was easier for him. Just because it was easy to believe, didn't make it true.

"I'm no killer, Tyrese."

"All of us are killers," he hissed, "If you can put a bullet between an Iraqi's eye, you can kill one of your own men."

"We swore the same oath," I uttered coldly.

"Someone has broken that oath. And it won't be the first time that you haven't kept your word."

My fists clenched against my will. Accusing me of murder was one thing, but disloyalty to my country? To the men who I'd served with? Tyrese's frustration was leading him to a personal attack and if he took things further, I didn't think I could control my response.

"I have never dishonored my country."

"You lied to me. You slept with the woman we are supposed to be protecting in clear violation of everything we both know to be true of these missions."

"That doesn't make me a traitor."

"That remains to be seen."

"I've had it Tyrese! You know me better than anyone. Why aren't you questioning Zhang? Or Ellis?"

"Because neither of those men were awake when Robert was dragged from his tent and massacred. That's why."

"Are you accusing me then? Are you going to keep eyes on me at every minute?"

"I'm going to do what I have to do."

"Fine. Then do it."

I stormed off back to camp where I grabbed the ax and began to split more wood for our fire. Tyrese ignored my angry demonstration and called both Zhang and Ellis aside to speak to them. I doubted that he would get very far with either of them. Aminata stared at me curiously from the corner of her eye when she thought no one was looking, no doubt intriguied about the content of my conversation with Tyrese. I had no good news for her, only bad blood. I knew Tyrese better than any of the other men on this journey and he knew me. The deaths had shaken him. He felt responsible, I knew that. He had always been a tough leader but he had never been unfair until now. This was only supposed to be a short trip.

All of us should I have already been home. Now, two of us would never make it. Both men had families. And kids. If I had been the killer, it would have been easier for Tyrese. That bastard should have known better than to believe I could do something like that. He knew me too well to have doubts. I didn't think I would get a moment alone with Aminata. Most of the day, none of the men had energy for month. Ellis and Zhang retired to their tents, sleeping off the pain of the fresh loss and salving their wounds with the rest of the whiskey. We'd run out of that soon too. Tyrese left to walk towards the beach and he begged Aminata to go with him but she insisted on remaining at camp with me. Tyrese didn't trust me, but Aminata promised that with a hunting knife, she'd be safe. I sat next to her on the log.

"He's been busting my ass since morning," I grunted.

"Vodka?"

"Where do you have vodka?"

She reached from inside of her fleece and pulled out a small flask. I drank without hesitating.

"You always have vodka available, don't you."

"I'm Russian," she replied, in a thick, Russian accent.

"Whoa. I don't think I've heard you talk like that before."

"There's a whole side of me that you don't know."

"Your Russian side?"

"Yeah. I guess it surprises most people. You know. I don't exactly look the part."

"No. You don't."

"I feel as Russian as any of my brothers. I suppose I was meant to have this life then, no? My parents were from the heart of Africa, both as black as you could imagine, but where did their daughter end up?"

"Life is funny like that."

"It is. I have to believe we'll make it off this rock alive."

"Rescue is on the way."

"I know. But do you believe we'll make it?"

I reached for her hand and squeezed it tightly. If she was afraid, she didn't show it. Amy had come to terms with a lot during our time holed up on this island. Where there was once fear, I found a fierce determination to survive. To make it.

"Of course I do."

"Do you really believe it, even with Robbie gone?"

"Yes."

"What did Captain Lorde say about Ellis?"

"He dismissed me. Immediately."

"Strange."

"I thought so too."

"Do you think he's hiding something?"

I hadn't been willing to consider that option. I trusted Tyrese like a brother. I trusted him with my life. While his trust in me might have wavered, I never for a second believed that he would work with a German biker gang.

"No. Tyrese is a man of his word. He would never kill a fellow soldier."

"But he is capable of killing?"

"Not all killing is the same," I responded, a little too brusquely.

She recoiled, taking her hand away from me.

"Sorry. I didn't mean to snap. I'm angry, that's all. Tyrese won't listen. Ellis and Zhang are a mess. I barely understand why all this is happening."

"Neither do I."

She leaned her head on my shoulder and I could smell her hair. Despite the sea salt, and questionable hygienic conditions, she smelled beautiful — like fresh flowers and sea salt. I kissed the top of her head.

"Aren't you worried Tyrese will see us?" I teased.

"I don't care. I don't care if he sees us at all. Who knows if we will see tomorrow?"

Despite her stiff upper lip, she was worried.

"I hate thinking this is all my fault," she confessed.

"It isn't."

"Of course it is! Without me, without me and my stupid posh life, none of us would be out here, stranded on an island, freezing our asses off and getting *murdered!*"

"The island has been getting warmer—"

"Oh Christ's sake, Mace. How can you be so casual?"

"I've stared death in the face, and I've never been scared of it before. The only difference now is that I actually have a reason to stay alive."

I brushed her hair out of her face and kissed her. And then, she understood. She kissed me back, running her hand over the prickly, irritating stubble that covered my face since we landed on this rock. Her lips were gentle, a tender reminder of what awaited me if we survived. If we made it, we could be together in the real world, not sneaking around in tents, not hiding from Tyrese or worrying about being killed.

"I love you," she whispered as she pulled away from me.

"I love you too."

"Is this all too crazy? How fast this happened?"

"Yes. But that's what I love about it."

I kissed her again. Crazy was my middle name. And Amy might have been insanely hot, the best kisser I'd ever met and have skin so flawless she belonged in a museum, but she was more than that.

"I want you to be my girl," I whispered.

She kissed me back and then she squeezed my hand.

"My tent. Now."

She was desperate for me, and hearing her beg for me sent a wave of relief over me. While Tyrese had his suspicions, the one person that mattered believed in me. Amy. Never for a second did she doubt my integrity as a man. She saw past my foul mouth, my drinking and the coarse way I interacted with my buddies. I could protect her. I could take care of her. She unzipped her tent and I followed her in, crawling over the tangled sheets, my cock rising in anticipation of our own entanglement.

She didn't want careful this time. Barely bothering to zip the tent shut, she got to work stripping my clothes off. The men could awaken at any moment or Tyrese could return to camp and find us pawing at each other's naked flesh, rutting and moaning in the cold winter air. She unbuttoned my shirt and tossed it aside, stripping off my undershirt and running her tongue down the length of my abs. Nasty. I liked it.

Watching her attack me with such furious desire drove me crazy. Once she had finished licking my rock hard chest, I pulled her face up to meet mine and planted a crazy, sloppy kiss right on her lips. She moaned as I kissed her and I shoved my tongue down her throat deeper…

Our tongues danced against each other as her hands hurriedly undid my pants, pulling them over my ass. She flopped onto her back, spreading her legs so I could press my full weight between them. Her thighs clung to my torso as I slipped her pants to the side and hastily shoved my entire length into her tightness. She was soaking wet, but the surprise entry of my cock surprised her sweet little cunt and she moaned as my length and girth stretched her to full capacity.

"OHHHHHH," she cried out, not caring about the noise she made or the fact that anyone could stumble upon us. I pressed my hand over her mouth instinctively and pumped hard between her legs. She whimpered, her breath hot and desperate against my palm as I shoved my cock deeper between her legs. She trashed about, her cunt dripping around my member as I continued to thrust into her madly. I'd never been so hungry for a woman's cunt before.

Hers was the perfect warmth and tightness. Her pussy clung to my cock, sucking it in deeper and gripping like a vice as I pounded between her legs, pleasuring every inch of her pussy. She moaned and came within a few moments of my cock's assault on her wetness. As she came, she hooked her ankles behind my buttocks, wrapping her body even tighter around me. We wouldn't have much longer before someone returned. I had to force myself not to be careful with her, to give her a hard and rough fuck before we put on a good face to the other men.

But oh, this minx was so good at playing innocent. I grunted as I plunged into her deeper and forced her to cry out again with another climax. She squeezed her eyes shut as her pussy clamped down around my dick tighter. I grabbed onto her hips with my free hand and guided my cock even deeper into her cunt.

"Cum for daddy," I growled as I watched her squirm and twist in pleasure beneath me. I pressed my weight into her harder, enjoying the force of pinning her down and using her sopping desperate cunt for my pleasure.

My rage at what happened to Chubb and Peña in addition to my frustration with Tyrese had pent up energy that needed release. I made love to her harder, pinning her down tightly as she squirmed and endured one relentless climax after another. She whimpered softly now as she had cum too much to sustain the energy to continue those desperate moans of hers. I released my grip on her mouth and trailed my hand down to her beautiful neck. I hovered over it, waiting for her to beg with that filthy mouth of hers.

"Choke me… daddy…" she pleaded.

Fuck. I would never get tired of hearing her beg for daddy's hand around her sweet little throat as I fucked her tight cunt. I wrapped my hand around her neck and squeezed as I entered her deeper. My tightness around her neck forced her to cum again and her nipples stiffened, poking through her fleece as she came this time. Her pussy juices soaked my thighs and the blankets beneath us as she came. Her sweet honeysuckle scent filled the tent and I couldn't stand not to cum inside those pink fleshy walls any longer.

"I'm cumming…" I grunted and I squeezed her neck tighter as I thrust inside her those last few magical times. I groaned as I released, the primal satisfaction of an animal in the throes of absolute euphoria. I released my grip on her neck as thick spurts of my cum coated the walls of her pussy. I leaned in as I finished inside her and whispered into her ear, "I have half a mind to impregnate that tight little cunt of yours…"

She moaned and shuddered in response, a pleasurable response to those naughty words. She wrapped her legs around me and held me tightly, still buried between her legs.

I would never get tired of having her close to me like this. I was sure of it. The unfortunate backdrop of the snowy island did nothing to change how I felt about her. I wanted a future with her, though thinking of a future while we were still fighting for our lives felt too premature. I had to keep her safe first. I had to earn her. A woman like Amy does't fall out of the sky like that too often. I'd gone years without meeting a woman like her and as for love? I'd given up on love as some high-school fantasy, something that existed for me only before I'd become a soldier. I'd forfeited my chance at love the moment I put a bullet between a man's eyes for the first time. Love happened for civilians, not soldiers.

Amy stroked my hair and when I pulled out of her, she wasted no time in nuzzling close to me. I was forced to pull away from her. I heard voices coming back towards camp and since finishing, I'd come to my senses. She might not care, but we couldn't be found like this. Tyrese would lose it.

I scrambled and got dressed and zipped her into the tent. By the time Tyrese came back, I sat on the log, tossing wood chips into the fire.

"Where is she?" He barked accusatorially.

"Her tent," I snapped, grabbing a half empty bottle of liquor and splashing a few drops onto my tongue.

"Tonight, you have first watch," Tyrese said, "We don't have much longer here and although I can't trust anyone, I have no choice but to trust you."

"Zhang's your first officer."

"I know my men, Mace. Zhang is hurting from Robbie's death. I don't want to give him the responsibility. He might not be on his A-game."

"Fine. I'll do it."

"I'll be sleeping with one eye open tonight."

"Yes, sir."

Bubba and Tim awoke, both red in the face from the cold. Liquor warmed them right up and Tyrese updated both of them on this plans for the night. We didn't have much longer until our help was on the way and my guess was Tyrese had specific orders about what to do with us until help arrived. The weather had improved significantly, and though it was still cold, we weren't quite freezing to death like when we'd first washed up on shore.

Later in the evening, Tim cleaned and prepared the meat while Ellis made a concoction he called "West Virginia Bisque" out of some of our provisions and the meat. Dinner boiled slowly and we all sat around the fire in silence for over an hour, only grunting and passing flasks of vodka around the circle. Every once in a while, Bubba would glare at me with his piercing blue eyes as if to say, "You're a dead man, Harwood."

If anyone was taking Robbie's death hard, it was him. Maybe it was the fight they had or Bubba being a crazy, country boy, but he had it in his head that I was responsible for Robbie's death and I could sense he wanted vengeance. We retired to our tents and to first watch earlier than usual. We had nothing to say to each other, and none of us dared to mention our second fallen comrade. Last week, all of us had been together, alive, talking about how we would spend the money.

There was no more guarantee that we'd make it home. Once loud snores erupted from the other tents, Aminata crawled out of hers and sat next to me on the log I pulled up to her tent for first watch.

"Hey," she whispered, wrapping her arms around mine and leaning on my shoulder.

I grunted in response, continuing to stare into the flames, ruminating on the men we'd lost.

"You look upset," she whispered.

I get it. She wanted to talk. She wanted me to listen to her and be there for her. After all, we knew the risks of any mission we signed up for. She was sheltered. She had been sheltered. But the more I thought about that, the more my mind settled on the unfairness of it. Why should Robbie die for a woman who had never known hurt in her life? Why should any of us? Why did some men do the dying while the real killers roam free, pulling triggers from boardrooms thousands of miles away? Shit, it's the type of stuff that crosses every soldier's mind once in a while.

And even if I knew it weren't her fault, thinking like that got me mad enough not to want to talk. She kissed my arm and I settled a bit. She kissed my cheek and that made it easier to be close.

"You have a lot on your mind."

"Yes."

"You miss them both?"

"Yes."

"I am sorry that they have died."

"I know."

"Mace?"

"Hm?"

She squeezed my palm.

"I am sorry for all of this. I know you will never say it to me, but this is all my fault. I'm sorry for how I was born. I'm sorry for how naive I've always been."

"It's not your fault," I assured her.

"It doesn't matter. Two men are dead."

"And more might follow," I grumbled.

She squeezed my hand tighter.

"It scares me when you say that."

"I know."

I kissed her hand and toyed with it in my lap. The flames spoke to me, dancing and flickering about, they reminded me that all of this would soon end, and even loving her would be dampened as quickly as a hot wood chip tossed into a snowbank would sizzle and fade. Loving her was temporary. It always had been. Thinking otherwise would make me foolish. Where had love ever gotten anybody? Chester loved somebody. He had a family. Kids. In our line of work, loving somebody meant leaving them behind. Better to walk out the door rather than having her endure me being lowered into a foreign, unmarked grave.

"Mace?"

"Hm?"

"What are you thinking? Talk to me."

"It's nothing."

I took another swig of vodka, trying to make my response to her more true.

"When we get out of here, where will we go?"

"The closest base is in the United Kingdom. London. The Embassy. Then you'll be flown back to Moscow and I suppose we head back into Dulles."

"Dulles?"

"Washington, DC. It's where we usually go."

"Oh."

She sighed and then continued, "I guess I assumed you would come back to Russia with me. Or… I would go to America with you."

"We can't do that."

"Why not?"

"I've got to head home. Get my life together. Figure out what to do with all this money."

"What about us?"

"What about us? I can't put everything on hold to be your manservant, Amy."

"I wasn't asking that."

"Weren't you? Let's face it. You're a princess and I'm one of your little foot soldiers, a willing sacrifice to preserve your royal blood."

"That's not true!"

"You said it yourself. Men have died because of you."

"Screw you, Mace…"

"If you want to be with me, this is it. This is the real me. People die, you get fucked up and then you fuck things up."

She pulled her hand away and gazed at the ground, forlorn.

"You're angry."

"Fuck yeah, I'm angry. And the worst part of it is, I want you to understand. But you can't. You don't know what it's like to lose everyone. All your friends. Every fuckin' friend you ever had."

"I can try to understand. You don't have to run away to do that."

"You don't get it. Staying close to me, I'm going to hurt you. Yesterday it was Peña, but one day it'll be me lowered into an unmarked grave."

"That's not true."

"It is. So it's better if we go our separate ways."

"Is that really what you want?"

"No. But it's the right thing to do."

"What about what I think?"

"Being with me is too dangerous. You've seen it for yourself."

"And I'm not afraid…"

I grabbed her hand and turned her cheek so she looked into my eyes.

"Listen to me, Amy. I can't help it. Everything a SEAL touch is bound to disappear. I can't have that happen to you. I wanted to dream about a life where we could be together, but it's impossible. You and I can never be together."

She scowled at me with a quivering lower lip before she wrested her hand away and stormed off into the woods.

"Amy!"

She started to run.

"Amy!" I called after her again.

Oh fuck…

"AMY GET BACK HERE!"

Shit. She was out of my line of sight and I only knew the general direction she'd gone. I hadn't thought she was serious. I ran into the woods, calling her name as I sprinted down the trail. She must have already veered off the path and I had no way of tracking her since there was hardly enough snow on the ground in the areas we'd been trampling on all day. I ran a few hundred more feet still screaming before I heard Tyrese's voice behind me, along with the other two men.

AMINATA

They didn't find me that night. I was lucky that it was so warm and that I was dressed well for the weather. I found cover near Ellis' secret hot spring and nestled there with the blanket I had wrapped around my shoulders when I left the tent. I didn't relax until I was sure their search had taken me far from my spot. I'd guessed correctly that Ellis wasn't likely to give up his secret bathing spot, and Mace would never believe that I'd come here.

Perhaps going there was foolish, but early in the morning, as the sun rose, I stripped off my clothes and jumped into the hot spring. My short time on the island allowed me to regain my Russian tolerance for frigid weather and gooseflesh barely prickled over my skin as I walked barefoot toward the edge of the spring. It went up to my shoulders and I sank my head beneath the water, my body warming up for the first time in a long time. This was perfect. I swam around the tiny pool, but I was too nerrous to wait there for very long. I didn't want Ellis finding me.

As I dressed and twisted my hair into a tight, low hanging bun, I decided the best course of action would be returning to camp. From my position of cover, I hadn't noticed how much the landscape had changed over night. Wind and tiny flurries of fresh snow had washed out my footprints and any traces of the direction from which I'd come. I wrapped my scarf around my head and trudged back in what I was certain was the direction I had come from. I walked for ten or fifteen minutes before I realized that I hadn't yet come to the path, and I should have seen it sooner.

The sun had just rose, and I'd walked so much that I'd started getting warm. I wasn't thirsty, thanks to some of the fresh snow that I'd gladly melted beneath my tongue. After another half hour of walking, where I doubled back and found myself no closer to the path, nor on familiar ground, I began to get hungry. I tried to remember some of what I had seen the men foraging for. I had been walking for an hour, when I saw a man leaning against a tree, wearing the blue SEAL's uniform.

"Mace?!"

He turned around and I still couldn't make out his face. The man waved. I breathed a sigh of relief. It was Tim. I ran toward him. He greeted me with his usually blank expression.

"Hello, Miss Usmanov," he said, bowing low and respectfully.

"Hi. I'm glad I ran into you. I'm trying to get back to camp."

"You're a long way from camp. We have been looking for you for hours."

"Where am I?"

"We are not too far. We can head back there together."

We walked for about ten minutes, but we didn't appear to be getting closer to the path that I recognized.

"Where's the path."

"Should be a few feet up. Sorry, I must have wandered pretty far looking for you."

"That's okay."

"Care to tell me what happened?"

I didn't know if I did. But we had nothing else to do but to walk together and make conversation.

"I got into a fight with Mace, that's all."

"Harwood? What kind of fight."

"Sort of… personal."

"Ah. I see. Mace struggles to get along with many people."

"Yeah. I've noticed."

"He is a good man. Brash, but he means well."

"I know."

"When we get off this island, everything will be better."

"I'd be crazy to disagree."

"It's amazing we landed here though. After an accident like that, we're lucky any of us made it."

"So you believe it was an accident?"

"Yes."

"What makes you so certain?"

After all that happened, I couldn't believe that Tyrese's First Officer was the one calling into question the story about the intent of the accident. Tyrese was convinced that none of this was coincidental.

"Why would someone sink us out here on purpose? I respect Captain Lorde, but his ideas about this are wrong."

"What about Robbie and Chubb?"

"I'm not convinced it isn't some kind of animal."

"Beheading them?"

"Surely a wolf could do that?"

I kept quiet. There was no way Tim could truly believe that. An animal couldn't sever a head or hang it from a tree without leaving bite marks. I'd seen the bodies myself and the memory of it was forever imprinted on my mind. There was no animal. A soldier couldn't be that naive, could he? I wanted to hurry and get to the path, before the isolation of winter made me even more paranoid.

We were still walking half an hour later.

"Tim, where are we? Are we close?"

He reached for the compass in his pocket.

"Shit…" he mumbled after staring at it for a while.

"What is it?"

"The damn thing is broken."

He smacked the glass and the needle spun around furiously.

"You don't remember the way back?"

"I must've taken a wrong turn about a mile up. I didn't want to worry you and figured I could find the way if we just kept walking."

"So we're lost."

"I wouldn't say that."

"Shit…"

"I've got enough in my pack to survive for the night. We'll find somewhere to set up and sit still until one of the others finds us."

"Will they be looking?"

"Sure they will. And they've got working equipment."

"It's probably best if we don't wander further," I replied weakly.

I was starting to get very cold. Tim found a patch in the woods and cleared out the twigs to lay out two sleeping bags. Without tents, we'd be forced to sleep on the bare ground which I'd already done for one night.

With the sleeping bags out, Tim gathered wood to build a fire. He refused to let me lift a finger to help, and dragged a thick log over for me to sit on. He had no weapons except his hunting knife, but it seems he didn't need it. Inside his backpack, he had enough food to carry us through the day.

With the fire built, he offered me a sip of the soup he'd made. It was delicious. Far better than the West Virginian concoction Ellis boiled up the night before.

"Where are you from, Tim?"

"Los Angeles."

"You always lived there?"

"I grew up in Pleasanton, California. But my family moved to Los Angeles when I was young."

"Were your parents immigrants?"

"All of us were."

His contradictory response made me believe that he had no real desire to talk to me. I didn't press him for further details. Tim asked if I thought I would be alright alone for a while. I nodded, and he left, promising to return with more meat. He told me to scream if I needed him as he wouldn't be going very far. I could handle that. He stalked off into the woods and I sat, staring into the mesmerizing flames. There's magic in sitting around a fire. Our ancestors evolved alongside the flames and now, we are exposed to them so infrequently that we often forget the joy, the warmth, and the mild dose of euphoria from staring at the flames lapping toward the sky.

I heard a coyote or a wolf howling far away. I couldn't help but remember the time father had insisted on taking me skiing in the mountains. His idea of fun had always been so extreme. I sat at the top of the hillside, crying as he begged me to follow him down. Eventually, he told me that the Usmanov's all had the strength of wolves and that without that strength, we would be finished. His speech, at the time, made very little sense to me but I knew I wanted to be a strong wolf like my father so I followed him down… down… down…

I must have been out for hours. When I woke up, Tim hadn't yet returned, and the fire had faded to a dull glow. I stoked it with more kindling and chips of wood I'd found around our campsite and then I searched through Tim's backpack for the flask of soup. As I peered inside the canvas backpack, I couldn't help but take note of Tim's supplies.

He'd left behind a flask of soup, a canteen, a tiny plastic bottle of vodka, and a small notebook in the main pouch. I glanced around, ensuring my isolation before I plucked the notebook from his backpack. I was only curious. He spoke so little that I thought maybe I could learn something about the man who had come from so far away to rescue me. I resented the notion that I was some kind of ungrateful spoiled princess.

The first two pages of the journal were written in German. I flipped through some of the pages, catching snippets of phrases. The content appeared mundane, but then it turned into lists of numbers and lists of random German words, all scribbled hastily across the pages. Was this his, or was it Ellis'? My stomach twisted into knots. I shut the journal and shoved it back into Tim's canvas backpack.

Tim was Korean. His last name was Zhang. He couldn't be worked for a German biker gang. I reassured myself that despite this strange discovery, Tim couldn't have had anything to do with what happened here. He barely believed that we were under attack. I couldn't gather my thoughts and decide what to do because Tim returned. I did my best to disguise my wild-eyed expression, but when I greeted him, I couldn't help but feel deep gnawing suspicion right in my gut.

He'd returned with one rabbit, already gutted and skinned.

"I figured you didn't want to see any of that," he commented.

He'd been right. I didn't think my stomach could take it.

"You been holding up okay?"

"Yes."

"You're quiet."

"I've been here alone. Guess I got used to it."

"Okay. Well I'll make some dinner. Does that sound good?"

I nodded and watched as Tim started cooking. He whistled as he worked, and I must have dozed off because the smell of his food hit me and all of a sudden, he was calling my name and handing me a bowl. I grabbed it, groggily, trying to shake myself awake. It was getting harder not to fall asleep. My day had been more tiring than I gave myself credit for.

I ate and then Tim cleared my bowl and suggested I head straight to sleep. I wrapped myself up in my sleeping bag, but I couldn't fall asleep so easily. Tim was whistling a familiar song to himself and my inability to place the song bothered me. Then there was the journal. I tried to keep what parts I'd read alive in my head. I had to admit that I hadn't read anything suspicious. The first few words I'd come across were benign.

But how strange was it, that he had this connection to Germany that I'd never known. He was elusive when I questioned him about his past. What if this kind, mild mannered man with the soft black hair and the wisps of stubble on his chin wasn't as innocent as he looked?

He had genuinely mourned when Robbie died. He gave a eulogy that wrenched my heart. He'd been surprised when Chubb's body was found too. No, it had to be a coincidence, or perhaps something he'd taken from Ellis. I couldn't believe that Tim Zhang was the man we were looking for. And with that comforting thought, I allowed myself to drift to sleep.

My thudding heart and a tightness in my chest thrust me out of slumber early, before the sun came up. Tim snored, loudly, and I wanted to reassure myself that nothing was wrong, I had no suspicions about him and I felt completely safe. My intuition had never lied to me before, however, and as I awakened, the sense gripped me that Tim had some explaining to do about the German journal in his backpack. I couldn't let him know what I knew, however. I had to act normal and be clever enough to survive. If Tim had killed those two men, trained Navy SEALs, he could kill me too. I doubted that Tim had ever planned to take me back to camp. The day prior, I'd been willing to give him the benefit of the doubt, but as morning crept up through the darkness, my suspicions grew.

When had any of the other men been lost? How could a Navy SEAL who had gone out to search for me have not realized what direction camp was in? I had those questions and many more about Chester and Robbie. If Timothy Zhang had killed both of those men in cold blood and managed to mourn at their funerals, he was a sociopath. If this was it, how I would meet my bloody end, I had to at least go out fighting. I snuck over toward's Tim's backpack, quieting my breathing and diminishing how much I crunched into the snow. This time, I searched the front pocket and stumbled upon a spare pocket knife with the initials RP carved bluntly into the side. Each of the men had taken tokens to remember Robbie by. This particular trophy sent chills down my spine. I swallowed a lump down my throat and shoved the knife into my pocket before I returned to my sleeping bag and closed my eyes until I heard Tim wake up. No matter how I tried, I hadn't managed to get back to sleep.

I listened to Tim get the fire going again and he hummed to himself as he sharpened his knife, and cooked some of the meat he'd slaughtered the night before for breakfast. I had to wake up eventually. I couldn't hide from him forever. I sat up and Tim greeted me with a warm smile. I searched his eyes for anything disingenuous, but that warmth was there — and it was real.

"Good morning, rise and shine!"

"Hey…"

"Want something to eat?"

I nodded and joined him near the fire. After a night of sleeping on the ground, even with a sleeping bag, I longed for the heat. He poured me some coffee in a small metal mug. For a man who had been spontaneously lost, he sure came prepared.

"Thanks," I muttered.

"Did you sleep okay?"

I nodded.

"Good. Looks like we missed sunrise."

"Yeah."

"I think we can try heading South again today. Hopefully we'll stumble upon camp then."

"Okay."

"Are you alright, Miss Usmanov."

"Why do you ask?"

My heart pounded as I white-knuckled the small metal mug.

"You seem tense."

"No. Bad back. From the ground."

"Ah, I see. You get used to it."

"I find that hard to believe."

"Trust me, it took me years."

"The SEALs?"

"Uh huh," he replied, crouching near the pot on the fire and stirring around the meat stew.

"How long have you been in the Navy?"

"Why do you ask?"

"Curious."

"Five years."

"Wow. And you're a SEAL already?"

"I underwent mandatory military service in Korea so I had some of the prerequisite training."

"We have this in Russia for men as well."

"It's good for you. Toughens you up."

"Some people think it's barbaric."

Tim shrugged.

"There's nothing barbaric about learning how to fight for your country."

"Yes, loyalty is important."

He raised an eyebrow and looked at me, but he didn't respond to my statement directly.

"You have three brothers, Miss Usmanov?"

"Yes."

"I heard talk that you were previously unaware of their underground activities."

"I wasn't. It shocked me. Although maybe it shouldn't have. Papa always kept these kinds of things away from me."

"Even as his daughter, you didn't know that your father was a criminal?"

His use of the word "criminal" seemed overly harsh. But then again, both Bubba Ellis and Chester Chubb had suspected they had similar amounts of respect for my father.

"As far as I knew, my father was a diplomat."

"An oligarch."

"Yes, something of the sort."

"And you… Did you ever wonder how an oligarch came to adopt you?"

I hadn't thought much of it. Papa had never hidden much about how he'd come to be my father. He'd grunt, and hem and haw, and explain that it didn't matter how, the fact was that he loved me and he always would. I knew that my biological father was under his employ, and that my mother was dead. What did it matter? To me, they were phantoms, missing pieces to a puzzle that I could never have hope of solving because everyone involved was dead.

I thought about them, but not often. I had Papa. And Papa was all I needed.

"Papa explained it to me," I told Tim.

"Hm. But still, doesn't it strike you as odd that your father never worried about you being collateral damage?"

"He always kept me safe."

"Good," Tim replied, "It's a dangerous world out there."

His words haunted me. Before I could respond, he offered me some of the stew he'd made for breakfast. I accepted a large bowl and by the time I finished eating all of it, I was exhausted. I let out a loud yawn.

"Is everything alright?" Tim asked.

"Mhm."

"You seem tired."

"I am."

"Why don't you rest a bit more. We will head out once you wake up."

I didn't understand why I had become so sleepy, but Tim's suggestion sounded fine to me. I crawled back into my sleeping bag, hardly remembering how I got there, and I fell right to sleep. I woke up with sharp tightness in my chest. It was dark.

"Hey, you slept in a long time. You must have needed it."

Tim. He sounded normal. Like I hadn't just slept through the entire day, and possibly more days. I sat up, groggy. What the hell had happened to me? As I shook myself awake, I tried to remember what I could. The stew. Tim's stew. That had to be it. He drugged me. My suspicions about him were confirmed with that realization. But it was cold. And dark. And I would never make it back to camp alone.

"Hungry?"

"We were supposed to head back to camp today."

"I know…But… you were sleeping. I didn't want to get you up."

I fumbled in my pocket for the pocket knife and my fingers found it. With shaking hands, I moved to pull it out.

"Cut the shit, Aminata," Tim said as he saw my hand reach into my pocket.

I froze.

"Huh?"

"Cut the shit. I already know you stole my knife and it won't make a difference. No matter how fast you run, I'll catch you."

I swallowed the lump in my throat and without thinking, I turned around and raced into the woods. My biggest comfort was the fact that Tim didn't have a gun, and it was pitch black. Once we left the fire, I didn't have to out run him, I just had to find somewhere to hide. I had nothing but the clothes on my back and the tiny little pocket knife, and not a single clue what direction our camp lay in. I ran fast and I could hear him slowly packing his things up.

"YOU CAN RUN BUT YOU CAN'T HIDE, AMY!" He called.

I kept running, knowing that I would have to stop, but that wherever I stopped, he could find me. If I closed my eyes even for a moment, he would find me. This man had tracked and killed two grown men who were each twice my size. Once he caught me, he could slaughter me like a pig. I ran for about a mile and I stopped, pausing against a tree. I couldn't let myself rest for long. Tim's confidence that he could catch me meant he hadn't raced after me right away but he was both stronger and faster than I was. I couldn't let my guard down until I found somewhere that I knew would be safe. As I caught my breath, I made a plan. Tim had seen me run one direction. Where I stopped, I gazed up at the stars, and used them for guidance. Papa had taken me out in the Ural Mountains many times before and forced me to look up at the sky and understand our universe. I knew enough to orient myself and figure out the last place Tim would expect me to go.

I moved East and the doubled back towards our old camp. This time, I couldn't run. Tim would be in these woods and he had the advantage of being faster than I was, quieter than I was, and whatever other training he'd received. Mace hadn't spoken to me much on his missions, but I knew he had killed before.

Thinking about Mace hurt like hell. He probably had no clue where I was, if he was even still on this island. Our last fight had been useless, frustrating, and a horrible way to say good-bye. I'd grown more cynical at the prospect of making it off the island goodbye. I couldn't accept that this was how my first great love would end. I cared about Mace more than I had any other man. Before we had the chance to test out the real world, everything had fallen apart.

I trudged through the snow, moving quietly through the dark, stopping every once in a while to listen to the stillness. My breath sounded like it was on a loudspeaker. I would have normally loved that deep silence that settles over a winter night. The quiet reminded me of Moscow, and of our country house. But here, quite only stimulated terror. If the silence broke, that would mean the end of things for me.

I stumbled back upon the camp Tim and I had made the night before. He'd covered up the fire a bit, but I recognized a few of the trees and the trampled earth. I didn't linger there for long, but skirted the perimeter, heading Southeast. Tim hadn't found me yet. I prayed for fresh snow that would cover my tracks more thoroughly, but thus far, I didn't have that kind of luck. Even if I lost Tim temporarily, without Mother Nature's help, he'd find me again. I kept walking past the camp, more careful than I'd been before. Seeing the sight where he drugged and threatened me sent me a grave reminder of the stakes. This was no simple walk in the woods.

I kept walking another few hours. I went slowly, taking my time to stop and listen, and make sure that at least for the time being, I was alone. Aside from the usual muffled chattering of critters and hooting of owls, I only heard one lone wolf uttering a funereal howl up to the crescent moon. I had to stop walking eventually, but I didn't relish being out in the open. I found a tree with a large trunk, that must have been hundreds of years old. It had been years since I'd climbed into a tree. But this had a branch just low enough that I could hoist my exhausted body up into it. I climbed up onto the thick branch and found a better place to sit a couple branches up. It was too dark to see very much ahead and I couldn't fall asleep, but I crouched up in the branch for an hour or so, leaning my head against the trunk.

My stomach growled with hunger, and I hadn't had any water in hours. I didn't want to leave the tree until day time when I had a better chance of being on equal footing with my pursuer.

I had the chilling thought that perhaps Tim hadn't pursued me at all, and he left me out in the woods to die. Unfortunately, the Germans wouldn't leave a job like this half-done. I couldn't allow myself to get too comfortable. As I waited until morning, I realized how far I'd come. When those men had broken into Feodor's apartment, guns blazing, I had never been filled with more terror. When I learned of my family's criminal history, I knew I could never survive in their world. But here, on this island, with Mace, I had found a survivor within myself.

You have to make it, I told myself. You have to.

By the time the sun crept over the horizon, I rested my legs enough to continue on. Adrenaline kept me awake as I shimmied down the side of the tree and scooped some fresh snow into my mouth. I no longer felt hungry, just a sharp pit in my tummy. I didn't have the energy to run any longer. Unlike the SEAL's, I hadn't trained for yers how to survive a night with little sleep. The drug induced sleep Tim had put me under hadn't been restful at all.

I walked for a mile or two before I couldn't stand my hunger any longer. I had to find something to eat, or I wouldn't make it. I was lucky enough to find blueberries, and I grabbed a handful, stuffing my face with them and squeezing them between my fingers until my hands were covered in sticky juices. I wiped my hand on my jacket after I ate, and continued my journey. After another mile, I came across the trail. Excitement surged through my chest. I'd found them again. Well, I'd at least found my way back. The trail I found was the East/West trail that Tyrese had cleared. I stumbled down past a few rocks and fallen logs to the trail. I walked a few feet before a sharp pain surged through my leg. I screamed and fell, face-forward onto the snow, too quickly for my hands to brace my fall. Before I could adjust to having fallen, my weight was swept out from under me and a large rope, dangled me upside down from a giant tree branch that ran just over the trail.

Tim had me in his snare.

I screamed and writhed, attempting to reach upwards to grab my leg and free myself from the unfortunate position. Adrenaline only surged faster and like every wounded animal, I yelled and struggled as I attempted to free myself. Camp was close by. Maybe Tyrese or Mace would hear me and free me from this mess.

"HEEELLLLLLLP!"

I shrieked over and over again as I reached up toward my ankle, flopping down and swinging from side to side, still yelling in frustration. If Tim hadn't realized I'd been caught yet, he'd figure it out soon. I didn't have much time. I couldn't possibly. After twenty minutes of struggling, I succumbed to my fate. I hung there by one leg, swinging from side to side like a helpless butchered pig in a meat shop.

When I saw Tim coming towards me, I hung limp. I'd been caught and there was only one way I could face my impending death. I wouldn't allow Tim to feast on my weakness, or derive pleasure from my captivity. He approached me with a smile on his face, as if everything was normal.

"I told you that I would catch you," he said calmly.

He set a large, closed bucket on the ground in front of me. I recognized it as the one he'd used to clean the meat from their hunts.

"What are you doing?"

"Don't worry Princess Usmanov. I am not going to butcher you. That is not the message that Herr Wagner wishes to send."

I maintained my stiff upper lip, refusing to dignify him with a response. He opened up the bucket and the unmistakable smell of freshly spilled blood hit my nostrils. Being nauseous upside down is one of the worst feelings, and I could only thank the heavens that I didn't upset my stomach.

"If I told you this was the blood of your lover, Harwood, would you believe me?"

I didn't respond, but he snickered anyway as if my silence was good enough for his amusement.

"It is his blood. I killed him and I killed Captain Lorde and I gutted them like pigs. Your father's debt must be repaid. It's nothing personal, I'm sure you understand that. Of course, after this, my career with the SEALs is done. Fun while it lasted. You know what I mean? It's better to be on the right side of the law. Easier. But it doesn't matter to me in the end, you know."

He reached into the blood with his bare hands and started to smear me in it. I squeezed my eyes shut and he chuckled.

"Don't worry, you don't have to look now. When I leave you here, every wolf in a ten-mile radius will be looking for you. I don't have to do the dirty work. All I have to do is sit back and watch. It might surprise you but I don't prefer that. I prefer getting into the action. But the boss was clear…"

He kept smearing my legs with the same unfettered tranquility one might have while seasoning a Thanksgiving turkey.

"I wish I could say I was sorry, Miss Usmanov."

He finished, ending by smearing my face with the stick, gelatinous blood.

"If you don't freeze to death, the wolves will get you. My job is to hang tight and see which happens first."

He admired his handiwork and then exhaled a sigh of relief.

"Well, that's done. I suppose I'd better get something to eat. I'll be back to check on you later."

He gave me a forceful push, sending me swinging across the path, blood oozing into my clothing and sliding down my skin, dripping into my eye and some of it slipping past my lips.

"Bye, Amy!" He called before he disappeared into the woods, whistling.

Part V

❧❦❧

MACE

She'd been gone for too many days. Tim had returned last night after a full day of looking for her. He told Tyrese that he found other footprints in the snow, another man's footprints. Perhaps we weren't alone on the island after all. We had been stalked, Tim supposed over supper, and whoever had arrived on the island with us had been picking us off one by one. Tyrese didn't buy his theory, and neither did I. For the rest of the day when we weren't looking for Amy, I kept a close watch on Ellis.

He didn't mind as he saw it as his opportunity to keep a close watch on me. We were mutually distrustful of each other which meant a lot of silence which meant a lot of time for thinking. I didn't believe that Amy had what it took to survive out here alone. That night, Tim had disappeared for a time to search for Amy again, but he arrived before we put the fire out to inform us that his search had been futile. He'd found more evidence of another man's presence on the island.

He handed Tyrese a black journal, filled with German phrase and Cyrillic codes. Tyrese seemed to believe that it was all the proof he needed, but Ellis eventually told me that Tyrese believed the journal belonged to one of us. That night, after dinner, Ellis kept first watch.

I couldn't manage to get to sleep knowing that Amy was out there, suffering in the cold somewhere and hidden well enough that with days of searching we'd been unable to find her. I joined Ellis on the log and gestured for him to pass the last remaining drops of vodka over to me. I couldn't smell vodka without thinking of her lips, the scent of her skin or how soft she was in my arms.

"Do you buy that shit about the journal?" Ellis murmured to me after a while.

"Hm?"

"Timmy and his German journal he handed to Tyrese."

"He found it out there. I have no reason to believe him."

Ellis shook his head.

"Something ain't right, Harwood. I don't trust that chink."

"You don't have to bring race into it, Ellis."

"Fine. Then I plain don't trust him. Does that make it more palatable for your liberal mind?"

He took another swig of vodka and handed the bottle back to me.

"It's all too convenient."

"You're a suspicious man, Ellis. Just the other day you were convinced that I killed Robbie."

"So fuckin' what. A man's allowed to change his mind."

"I find it hard to believe Tim is capable of doing all this. I mean look at him, he's Tim."

"Right. The reluctant soldier. The stoic. Lemme tell you something, Harwood. All men are the same. We all have a thirst for blood. Some of us have it stronger than others, is all."

"I doubt that person is Tim."

"Suit yourself. I won't try to change your mind. All I'm saying is I don't trust the motherfucker."

None of us trusted anybody out of any other reason than necessity. We all assumed that we needed the rest to survive here. Of course, that wasn't exactly true as all of us except Aminata had the training to make it in these woods. If she was still alive, she wouldn't be for very long. I resented Tyrese's order to call off the search for the day. She hadn't wandered far… Where on earth could she be now?"

Thinking about her kept me up until the end of the first shift. I got up and Tim stood guard. I slept horribly. Memories from Iraq and Syria flashed inside my head as if they were nightmares and not real events. Severed heads. Extreme hunger. Thirst beyond any that I'd known. Every horrible thing I had been exposed to during my career now came bubbling up to the surface of my consciousness. Before I awoke, my memories were only about Amy. Amy's hair. Amy's smell. The way she spoke with that technically correct but somehow imperfect accent that most foreigners have. I missed the way she tipped vodka back into her throat and winked at me as she swallowed without wincing.

In the morning, Tyrese's voice echoed through the camp. I unzipped my tent and stood outside, alone. After a few of Tyrese's short yells, neither Ellis nor Zhang emerged from their tent. Tyrese yelled their names sharply. I stood at attention, staring straight ahead, Tyrese's mounting anger not lost on me.

"ZHANG!"

"ELLIS!"

…

…

"Harwood. Open up these tents for me."

I unzipped all the tents and Tyrese walked toward each one, ruffling the sheets and finding all of them empty.

"Where are these men…"

"I don't know, sir."

"If I walk around these woods, will I find these men dead, Harwood?"

"I don't know, sir."

"Don't you?"

"I don't appreciate the implication, sir," I uttered resentfully through gritted teeth.

"I don't need to explain to you why I don't believe you, Harwood. We'll talk about that later. Let's do a sweep of the woods so I don't make a fool of myself."

My gut told me that we wouldn't find either of the men. We

walked around the first half mile radius of camp, taking over an hour to do it. My stomach growled, and my body yearned for a sip of coffee, whiskey, or the unholy mixture of both of them. Tyrese didn't betray any exhaustion. We cut through the brush until we'd finished one sector of our search. There were no signs of either of the men. No signs of anyone.

Tyrese turned to me, the silence of winter chilling his already icy expression.

"Where. Are. They. Harwood."

"I don't know, sir."

"Harwood, we're going to have some problems if you don't tell me the truth. You're the only one left and I know that I didn't make these two men disappear. Therefore, it has to be you. Where are they."

"Damn it, Tyrese. I have nothing to do with their disappearance."

I was too frustrated with him for respect, and rank and hierarchy. I had nothing to do with the two men going missing and I had just as much of a reason to suspect Tyrese as he had to suspect me. Perhaps working with Aminata was just a pretext to cover up his own actions. I already knew that he owed a favor to one of the most terrifying gangs in London. If he was in bed with one group of gangsters, what was stopping him from getting into bed with another set of 'em?

"Why are you the only man alive then? Do you have another theory?"

"Yeah. I do. Maybe you killed them."

"Are you saying I betrayed my country?"

"You're the only one of us who's been in bed with thugs and gangsters before…"

"Are you saying I betrayed the United States?" Tyrese roared.

"Maybe I am!"

Tyrese yelled and swung at me. He dropped his knife, preferring to use his fists as he pummeled me. He had the element of surprise on his side, and to be honest, the element that I didn't want to fight one of my superiors. Once he took the first hit, all bets were off. I hit back. Hard. After a few more hits, Tyrese started going mad. He had me on my back and try as I might have to push him off, he had a little extra motivation to keep me down. He really believed I killed those men. I didn't assume his guilt. He grabbed his knife and pressed it to my throat.

"Careful, Mace. You're fucking with the wrong guy."

"If you think I did it, slit my throat," I spat, "Kill me right here. Tyrese we're brothers! We're fucking brothers…"

His hand shuddered as he gripped the knife handle. The cool blade pressed against my throat as I became ever more cognizant of blood coursing through the veins on my neck. Tyrese pulled the knife away at the last second.

"I'm giving you the benefit of the doubt. Get up. Let's go back to camp and we'll talk about this."

"Okay. Okay."

I got up, wheezing, but glad that I hadn't ended up with my throat slit over my loud mouth. Tyrese kept his knife pointed at me and I walked with my hands up in silence all the way back to camp. At camp, we had no fire any longer. Tyrese sat me down on a log and came back with zip-ties which he used to fasten my hands behind my back. He tipped whiskey to my lips.

"Drink."

"Sir, I don't know what you hope to accomplish," I remarked after I'd swallowed enough whiskey to get me properly drunk.

"I want you to admit the truth."

"You're going to torture me until I tell you, is that it?"

"I am using methods approved by our government to extract information from a suspect. This is under my jurisdiction…"

"This seems right to you?"

"Quiet, Harwood. It's time for me to ask you some questions. I want you to be honest with me."

"I have always been honest with you, sir."

"It's time for you to be even more honest, then."

Tyrese crouched in front of me, scrutinizing my face.

"What can you tell me about Chester Chubb's death?"

"Sir, you were there when we found him. I was shocked. Bewildered. I knew I had to start taking this mission seriously because there was somebody who could do that to a man lurking amongst us."

"Why were you so convinced it was one of the other men?"

"It didn't make sense it would be anyone else."

"Who did you suspect?"

"Nobody, sir."

"You didn't have any suspects?"

"No, sir."

"That hardly makes sense. How could any of the men have done it if you couldn't even suspect which one?"

"Sir, many people are able to be a wolf in sheep's clothing."

"Interesting that you say that, Mace."

"Why is that interesting, sir?"

"Nothing."

Tyrese paced back and forth a little longer.

"What is your connection to Aminata Usmanov, Harwood? Why bother get close to her? Why bother soil the oligarch's daughter if for no other reason than to humiliate him?"

I was too angry to answer him. I had no intentions of "soiling" Aminata or using her. He had no right to make these false accusations and then talk about her as if I saw her as an object or some prize to be won. I had never felt so deeply about a woman before and I couldn't avoid snapping if he pressed me further.

"Where is she, Harwood? Did you kill her too? Did you take her body out into the woods and cut her up like you did to Robbie?"

"I never killed Robbie! I never killed Amy! I NEVER KILLED THEM."

"You seem awful hot under the collar for someone who ain't guilty."

"Screw you, Tyrese! You fuckin' know me. You know I could never do that to someone. You know it!"

Tyrese landed a punch across my face. Hot blood trickled out of my nose as my cheek throbbed in pain. I didn't turn my face away from him. One blow wasn't enough for me to cower in fear before him. Tyrese might have been certain of my guilt, but I knew the truth, and I couldn't allow him to waste time questioning me when the killer was out there in the woods. We didn't have much time before help arrived.

"Prove it, Mace! Say one thing that would prove to me that you didn't kill the rest of our men and Oleg Usmanov's daughter. Help me to help you."

"I didn't kill her," I gasped, spitting out a wad of blood from my mouth.

"I didn't kill her. I love her!"

"You disrespectful sonovabitch," Tyrese growled. He punched me in the face again.

"Tell the truth!"

"I love her!"

"TELL THE FUCKIN' TRUTH."

"I ALREADY TOLD YOU."

Tyrese whipped his knife out of his pocket and he slashed it through the air swiftly. It took me a few moments to realize what he'd done. I felt the warmth first, intense heat like touching your hand to the side of a warm bowl of soup in winter, spread throughout the side of my head. Then I heard a loud popping sound and felt the blood.

My stomach churned as Tyrese pulled his hand away from my head, holding onto my severed ear. I tried to stay awake, to remember my training. I'd never been happier for the whiskey warming my stomach.

"We'll talk later today."

"I need a towel, Tyrese. If I bleed out, I'll die."

"Talk. Tell me something useful."

"I'll tell you who Aminata suspected."

Tyrese raised an eyebrow.

"Who?"

"Ellis. She suspected Bubba Ellis. She saw his German tattoos and she knew he was planning to kill her. You let him go. You let him run all over these woods while you fuck me up. He's probably killed her already. You might as well let me die 'cause I wouldn't want to face Oleg after killing his only daughter."

Tyrese growled and tossed me a towel.

"Don't worry. I won't let you die. I want Oleg to take care of you himself."

Tyrese wandered off to hunt and presumably continue his search for Zhang and Ellis' bodies, leaving me tied up. Getting out of zip ties was tough. A part of Tyrese must have believed that I wouldn't even try to escape. He was dead wrong. Amy was out there, she had to be. And I didn't believe that Ellis or Zhang was dead either. Maybe Tyrese and I both had it wrong and those two bastards were working together. Either way. I didn't want to wait around and find out. I figure my first order of business might be to wait until Tyrese returned. He would have to build a fire, he would have to cook food and he would have to get close enough to me to change the dressing on my ear. I'd have to strike then. I'd have one chance with Tyrese. If I messed up, he'd kill me. I heard Tyrese whistling about a mile off. I'd lost enough blood that I started to feel woozy. I had no choice but to keep my wits about me, despite the ringing in my ear that got louder as Tyrese drew closer to me.

He approached camp with something in his hand. At first, I thought it was an animal but as I got closer, I noticed the human eyes, snapped open and frozen that way. Tyrese set Ellis' head on the ground in front of me where I sat, his cold blue eyes staring back at me from the severed head.

"I found his body three miles up."

"Fuck…"

"I couldn't get the body back on my own but I wanted to at least bring his head back. Animals got to the rest of it… but he's still too heavy."

"I can help you if you let me."

Tyrese glowered at me.

"Look at him, Harwood. Stare into this dead man's eyes and tell me the truth. Did you kill him?"

"No, sir."

"Fucking hell, Harwood. This would be so much easier if you were just honest."

"I can't confess to a crime I didn't commit, sir."

"How's that ear?" Tyrese asked, or threatened. I was too out of it to care.

"Not good."

Tyrese removed the towel and touched his fingers to the congealed blood on the side of my face.

"You'd better eat and get some water in you. I'll clean the wound."

His mercy didn't impress me. I knew how the SEAL's worked. He had to keep me alive and healthy enough to withstand another bout of torture. I wouldn't have my second ear by this time tomorrow if I was lucky enough to survive the night. But last I checked, tomorrow we would have help. That meant I didn't have much time to find the others.

Patience was hard. Tyrese set up the fire and put on a pot of food. While he waited for his stew to cook, he dressed my ear. He undid my binds and waited with his knife out while I finished eating. When he came to get the bowl from my hand was my last time to strike. I fumbled, and instinctively, he stuck his hands out to catch the metal bowl before it hit the ground. Big mistake. I stuck my knee out and caught him in the chest. He let go of his knife as he doubled over. I grabbed the knife and landed another kick in his chest to make sure he was down.

"Bastard! I knew you killed them!"

"Shut up, Captain."

"Kill me! Kill me and be done with it, you coward!"

"Sorry, Tyrese. I told you that I didn't kill them and I meant it. But I've got to prove it to you and I don't have much time. This will be much easier."

"This insubordination will be punished! They'll put you to death for treason!"

I ripped my belt off and tied a tight knot around Tyrese's wrists, cinching them together. Keeping the knife pressed against his back, I led him to one of the tents and shoved him inside. Once he was inside, I fastened his feet together with another tie, holding him down as he kicked and squirmed, hitting me in the ribs or jabbing me in the thighs. He was strong, but this time, I was determined. If Amy was alive, I didn't think she would be for long.

Ellis was dead. That meant Amy and I had been wrong. In fact, Bubba was the only one who had suspected the truth: Tim Zhang had done this. He'd killed us all one by one, skirting past suspicion with his calm demeanor and his lawful appearance. I understood what kind of man I was dealing with the minute Tyrese had returned to camp holding Bubba's head. Tim was more cold-blooded than any of us could imagine. And it was safe to assume that he had Amy captive.

I had nothing but the knife I'd taken from Tyrese and the clothes on my back. I didn't need much more. My wounds had been dressed recently enough that I could ignore the throbbing in my head and the dull taste of metal beneath my tongue as I ran off down the path. I started at a slow jog to get my mind working and warm up my muscles.

Where could Tim have taken her? If she was alive, where the hell could she be? Tyrese had found Ellis' body three miles away. It stood to reason that Amy might not be far. For a moment, I'd thought of it as "Amy's body" might not be far, but I dispelled the thought. She couldn't be dead. I loved her. She was the type of woman that could make me forget that plenty of people I'd loved had died, and my loving them hadn't made them any better off. Amy dispelled my militaristic cynicism and as I ran, I thought about what it would feel like to hold her again.

Without the drive to protect her coursing through my veins, I might not have made it all three miles within thirty minutes. Without much food in my system, and with the amount of blood I'd lost, a regular man wouldn't have made it. I kept up my brisk pace, following Tyrese's tracks until I came to a darkened portion of the snow. I had about 45 minutes until sunset which would make hunting down Amy even more difficult. I stumbled upon Ellis' body by accident. I heard more animals than usual chattering and breaking twigs. I moved slowly through the trees and saw a large male bear shaking meat between his teeth. After a few moments of struggling to think of an animal as large as the one the bear ate, I realized that the bear had no animal between its teeth, but Bubba Ellis. I waited for the bear to wander off, longer than I'd liked but based on the sun's new position, I'd waited no more than 15 minutes. I wandered through the woods, calling for both Tim and Amy. I was prepared to deal with either one of them although due to my weakness, running into Tim would mean he had an advantage. I wandered around until the sun had settled into dusk. My voice was hoarse with calling Aminata's name when I heard a scream that could have only been hers.

"AMY!"

"AHHHHHHH!"

"AMY, IT'S MACE. WHERE ARE YOU."

"M-MACE!"

I ran towards the sound of her voice. I'd never run faster. I ran fast enough to forget the horrible throbbing on the side of my head and the paper dryness of my tongue. I ran until I came to a large body, suspended from a branch, hanging over a path that we'd cut out so many days ago upon first arriving on the island. As I approached, I realized the body hanging from the tree was Amy's. But she hung upside down, coated in congealed, partially frozen blood.

I couldn't tell if her response was due to the shock of seeing me, or if she had held out as long as she could and I'd just been lucky. I cut her down. She was cold… Too cold. And the blood on her face stank to high hell. I'd seen a bear not too far off too. As I cut her down, she lay there limp. I wouldn't be able to wake her up if I tried. I grunted and lifted Amy off the ground, slinging her over my shoulder and I trudged through the woods, beginning the long walk back toward camp. I couldn't get there in one night, especially not with Tim in the woods somewhere. If there were any chance he'd been killed too, I would have stumbled upon him somewhere in this radius. When Amy woke up, I'd have to ask her.

It wasn't safe for me to keep walking much longer than the two miles I walked with her along the trail. I wandered off the trail, marking trees with deep knife gashes as I went. Though Amy might have been cold, I no longer had to worry about that. My mouth was even more parched than before when I found a place to stop near some running water. Using what I could from the environment, I fashioned a vessel to get the water hot and built a small fire. I couldn't risk keeping it on for long, but I had to sponge the blood off Amy's exposed skin and clothes. She didn't wake up as I cleaned her and her clothing, sponging them off with a ripped piece of fabric from my shirt. By the time I was done, I barely had the energy to drink some water, tip some down her throat and turn the fire off. We'd have to wait until morning to move again. Right now, we had to stay still… Very still. I didn't dare sleep.

About halfway into the night, Amy finally roused from sleep. For a moment, she was terrified, as if reliving some past horror that had occurred while we were apart. She realized it was me and she leaned back, sighing with relief.

"Oh Thank God. It's you."

She closed her eyes and for a moment, I thought she was asleep again until I heard quiet sobs.

"Hey. It's okay. I'm here."

She clutched at me for a moment and kissed the top of my forehead before pulling away.

"I'm fine. It doesn't matter because I'm fine."

"Who did this to you, Amy. I need to hear you say it."

"Tim. All of it was Tim Zhang…"

"Shit."

"Are Officer Ellis and Captain Lorde alive?"

"The Captain's alive."

"Shit."

"We have to stay here until dawn and stay quiet. After that, we'll be heading back to camp."

"How far away are we?"

"A couple miles."

"I didn't walk it."

"No. I carried you."

"Mace…"

"Shh," I whispered, "All I need you to do is make it out of here alive."

She squinted as her eyes adjusted to the dark.

"What happened to your…"

She reached out to touch my ear and her hand recoiled as she touched the blood on my jagged flesh.

"My God, Mace…"

"Courtesy of Captain Lorde as punishment for your murder."

"No…" she whispered. She leaned her head into my chest and resumed her quiet sobbing.

"This is all my fault. For being naive. For being so stupid…"

"It's not your fault, Amy. You didn't choose any of this. Remember that."

I held her until she stopped crying. I soothed her enough to get her to sleep. I held Aminata's head, whispering that I loved her as she slept. I couldn't have fallen asleep if I wanted to. She woke up close to dawn, maybe an hour or so before the sun came up over the horizon.

She wanted to get started before dawn and despite the dangers, I admitted that the sooner we returned to Tyrese, the better chance we would have of finding him alive. We were careful as we walked through the woods. Still, Amy didn't have the same training that I did. She wasn't dead silent and I could hear her breathing as if the sound were coming from my own mouth. If Tim were close, he could track and catch us. Tim had caught Amy in a snare, but he couldn't catch me. Instinct guided my steps and I kept us clear off the path so our tracks could be easily hidden by the thick blanket of leaves on the ground.

Some of the snow had melted, but I hardly noticed the warmth. I noticed the sound of water. Where the forest had been silent, tiny streams of snowmelt cut through the leaves and formed tiny vernal pools and their own network of small rivers. Mud would make us easier to track but I held out hope that the water would block out the sound of Aminata's footsteps. Our luck was finite.

Tim might have had the element of surprise work to his advantage if he hadn't scared a bird off a few feet back, causing the dove to screech as it took to the skies, and alerting me to the truth that we weren't alone.

"Still, Amy," I whispered, placing a hand on her shoulder as I stopped, and listened.

A knife came whizzing past my hear, embedded in the side of a tree. Amy gasped and clasped her hand over her mouth to prevent screaming. I searched for Tim in the trees. Then I found him, the tip of his boot sticking out from behind a trunk. He wasn't doing his best job to hide.

"I can see you, Tim!" I called, "Get the hell out here and fight me like a man."

His boots crunched against a twig. Aminata whimpered, but reached for the ground and picked up a branch large enough to hit Tim over the head if she had the good luck to get close enough to him.

"Get behind me," I growled.

She listened, now more aware of the danger she was in more than ever. Tim stood about thirty feet off, his hands raised in mock defeat.

"You've got me, Mace," he chuckled, "I've been hiding out in these woods for days, trying to find Ellis. She must have told you about him, right?"

"I know Ellis is dead."

He kept walking toward me. 20 ft… 10 ft… Close enough for me to see the dark bags under his eyes from lack of sleep and the blood caked under his fingernails, likely from his earlier snare job with Amy.

"Dead? No way."

"I know you kidnapped Miss Usmanov."

"What? Mace, this must be some kind of mistake."

His tone never wavered, almost like he believed his own bullshit.

"Quiet, Tim."

"I'm telling you, Harwood, there must be some kind of mistake. Let's go back to camp and talk to Tyrese…"

He thought I was that stupid, huh? I always knew Tim resented me for being brash, impulsive and rough around the edges. I guess he thought I was just a dumb brute who he could manipulate the same way he manipulated our superiors and the officers that entrusted their lives to him.

Let's see just how stupid this brute can be…

I swung my fists. Amy screamed, but it was too late. I had Tim on the ground and I gained the upper hand. Bam! I slammed my fist into his face. For Chester. For Robbie. Even for goddamn Ellis. His face and my fists caked with blood. He sputtered and coughed but my assault didn't faze him. Tim laughed. He laughed as I hit him. He laughed, coughing and spitting up blood. Then he went berserk. He yelled loud and primal and pushed me off of him.

I went flying as Amy approached and attempted to swing her weapon at Tim's head. He blocked her once, twice, and then she swung lower, hitting his ribs and distracting him just enough that I could get the upper hand again. I grabbed his waist and slammed Tim onto the ground. Amy dropped her weapon, horrified at what she had done.

"That's enough, Harwood!" Tyrese's voice boomed as he approached me laying into Tim.

Despite the heat of the moment and my desire to make Tim pay, my instinct was to obey my superior. I dropped Tim on the ground as he grunted and chuckled.

"Sir, Miss Usmanov will tell you what happened to her."

"It's okay, Harwood. I believe you."

Tyrese walked over to Amy and touched her on the shoulder.

"You okay?"

She nodded, "It was Zhang… Tim Zhang."

Tyrese nodded and muttered something to her, giving her hand a gentle squeeze.

"We need to take him back alive," Tyrese informed me, "Oleg Usmanov has arranged a deal and he'll be going back to Russia."

"Sir, what about an arrest?"

"Don't worry about that, Harwood. Now come, help is almost here."

The sound of helicopters roared overhead a few minutes later. Rescue had finally come.

AMINATA

"Papa will see you now," Feodor uttered. He couldn't stop staring at me as I'd landed from an alien planet. He hugged me and kissed my forehead, flashing a grimace at Mace as he walked down the hallway back to his study.

"Are you ready?" Mace asked, reaching for my hand.

I shook my head.

"No."

"I promise, it will be okay."

He kissed my cheek and I knew he was right. The helicopter had taken us to Iceland first, the closest landmass. I'd been in the hospital in Reykjavik for a week, but due to a previous incident with the Icelandic government, Papa couldn't visit. He sent Boris first, and my brother muddled through our first meeting and what had actually happened since they'd lost track of our ship. Boris spent many hours on the phone with Papa, quarreling in Russian outside my hospital door nearly the entire time.

Papa made life a living hell for the Icelandic doctors from a distance. He worried about me so greatly, that he even tore into Boris, who barely caught a wink's sleep. Failing to miss one update to my father would send him into a series of aggressive tirades. Papa at first wanted all the men dead. In my weakened state, I spoke to him myself. He wept when he heard my voice and begged me to return to Moscow soon.

I couldn't bring myself to respond lovingly. Papa had lied to me my entire life. I couldn't simply return to Moscow and pretend the entire thing had never happened. While I was in Iceland, Tyrese and Mace returned to the United States to give updates on the situation that had transpired in The Atlantic. Mace promised at my bedside he would return. Boris didn't understand enough English to glean the content of our conversation, but when Mace kissed my forehead he was suspicious.

Boris questioned me, but I didn't relent. This wasn't Feodor or Vasily. I had no trouble lying to Boris. It didn't hurt that he was particularly naive compared to the other two. When Mace left, I hadn't expected him to return. Three days later, he returned. He'd been paid, and handsomely too as I understood it. By the time he returned, I was mostly recovered and when we saw each other for the first time, I couldn't help myself. I kissed him, and then Boris understood.

As soon as Mace left the room that first time, Boris returned with a scowl. He asked me (in Russian), "What was that all about?"

"It's complicated."

"I need to report this to Papa."

"No!"

"I must. You are consorting with an American soldier. Did he rape you when you were captive?"

"No! Boris, calm down. I… I love him."

Boris scowled.

"Please, Boris. Don't say anything. Papa will be furious if I don't explain this."

I eventually convinced him to be silent. My trepidation about seeing my father only increased when I Mace and I flew to Moscow. Boris insisted on sending a private jet for us, and I was pleased to have the freedom it offered to discuss what would happen next with Mace. At first, there had been awkwardness as we glimpsed for the first time what life might be outside of mere survival.

He held my hand as we descended onto my father's private strip in Moscow.

"We made it, nothing else matters now."

Walking into Papa's office, I didn't believe that nothing else mattered any longer. Papa peered over his spectacles, a hand-rolled cigarette hanging from his lips. He grunted and gruffly tapped the cigarette before extending his arms wide. He ignored Mace's presence entirely. I hugged Papa for the first time and my fears melted away. Papa might have been harsh and I could have surely accused him of being distant, but he was my father… He had chosen to be my father, and our bond could transcend even the lies he'd told.

"I'm sorry," he murmured, the Russian words caressing me with their warmth and familiarity.

"Papa…"

"I'm sorry for lying to you," he said, "I was only trying to keep you safe."

I'd never witness Papa betray emotion, but he choked back tears as he held onto me. I couldn't stand to do anything but to forgive him.

"Never lie to me again."

"My beautiful daughter… I have learned my lesson."

"Papa, I brought someone to introduce to you."

"Hmph."

"This is one of the soldiers that saved my life. He is the officer who saved my life."

Oleg grunted and nodded.

"Papa!"

He stuck out his hand and Mace shook it with a strong, firm handshake that I'd warned him not to mess up. Papa softened once he felt the strength in Mace's palm.

"Nice to meet you again, sir."

"Hm. Yes. Welcome to Moscow."

"Beautiful city, sir," Mace responded, resorting to his military honorifics as a nervous habit.

"Moscow? It is shit."

An awkward tension hung in the air for a few moments, with Mace utterly lost as to how to respond. Papa burst into laughter, enjoying the squirming and uncertainty. Mace cracked a smile and Papa thumped him on the back.

"Are there no jokes in America? Come. We will all have dinner tonight. Feodor and Vasily are back from Berlin. We have much to celebrate."

I didn't ask Papa what my brothers were doing in Berlin, and he didn't offer any answers on his own.

"Now my darling. It is good to see you, but I must work. Take the keys to the Maserati — the red one — and show this young man around."

"Yes, Papa."

We took our leave of Papa's office, and I took the keys from his silver box to the car key labeled Klubnika. I drove Mace around our neighborhood, and then towards our house. His eyes widened when he saw the stone house.

"Jesus Christ…"

"What?"

"This house is huge."

"All of us live here. It is more an estate."

Mace chuckled.

"You don't even know how insane you sound, huh?"

I loved being at home. Everything about the stone house brought me closer to forgetting the fear and the terror I'd felt about my life, and the desperate struggle to survive. Our doorman, Sergei, opened the door and took our coats. Mace's eyes continued to roam around the foyer. I welcomed the warmth. Ana emerged with her uniform to show us to our suite. My old quarters were intended for living alone, and this new part of the house had been updated, a fact which Papa was happy to show off. As we settled in, I heard a knock at the door. I recognized him before he spoke.

"Vasily!"

The door swung open and I rushed into my older brother's arms. He spoke to me in English, politeness that most of my family didn't offer Mace. His English had improved immensely since the time we last spoke.

"I'm glad you are alive, despite your best efforts."

"I missed you."

I didn't think I would ever see my closest brother again and thoughts of him had kept me motivated through the long cold nights. He extended his hand to Mace.

"I heard you are the man who kept my sister alive."

"I did the best that I could."

Mace shook his hand and Vasily smiled.

"I see you two are enjoying the new space."

"Yes, sir. It's quite comfortable."

"No sir, Vasily," my brother corrected him. I started to think they'd get along just fine.

"Have you seen Feo?" Vasily asked.

I shook my head.

"Hm. He should be around the estate soon."

"Speaking of Feodor, what were you two doing in Berlin?"

"These are not matters for women to trouble themselves about."

I folded my arms and spoke sternly to my brother, with an intensity forged in the forests of that wooded island of ice.

"I've been through more than enough hell to hear about family business and Papa has promised me no more secrets. I have starved. I have been captured. And I demand to know what you were doing in Berlin."

Vasily grimaced at Mace, "Do you know what you're getting into with her?"

"Vasily!" I exclaimed, smacking my brother on the arm.

"Fine. We were taking care of business pertaining to your capture."

He knew it wasn't enough to satisfy my curiosity.

"Fine. We are planning our revenge on the scorpions who killed soldiers and very nearly killed our sister. They made a mistake allowing us to find out who was behind what happened."

"You mean Tim?" Mace asked.

Vasily nodded.

"Tim's connection to the scorpions allowed us to breach some of their defenses. A man, part of a network of Parisian billionaires who develop real estate in South America, had been paying out the money to Tim's account. This man has a second cousin who was married off into the Wagner family."

"The biggest crime family in Germany."

"For now," Vasily replied.

Vasily's chilly response sent a shiver down my spine. While I had time to adjust to the news about my brother's secret activities, I hadn't grown accustomed to the casual nature with which they spoke about dispatching their enemies. The island might have hardened me, but I still had my sense of right and wrong.

"You are not going to kill innocent people, are you?"

Vasily grimaced.

"I told father this might not be such a good idea," he mumbled.

Mace dragged him back on topic, "In Germany, what happened once you found the connection?"

"We have ascertained the identity of the leading Wagners who recently, thanks to our brother, Feodor, had gone into hiding."

"What did Feo do?"

Vasily sighed, "I have a lot to catch you up on."

A loud doorbell rang throughout the suite.

"Papa is home," I whispered, smiling. I was home. Papa was home. My normal might have changed, but the familiar sounds and sights of my childhood made me feel safer. Maybe one night, I'd be able to sleep through the night without waking Mace, or waking up dripping in sweat and screaming.

"Perhaps I should go speak with your father. Give you time to catch up."

Vasily and I nodded, appreciating the gesture. With Mace out of the room, Vasily requested to practice his English.

"What really happened in Germany, Vasily. Did you kill anybody?"

"You think I can stand the look on your face when you find out the type of man I am?"

"I know now. I understand."

"No," Vasily replied harshly, "Papa told you what little he could get away with. You don't know the details of how I was raised. You don't understand how Papa turned us all into little soldiers."

"Are you angry with him?"

"Only for creating this mess and nearly getting you killed."

"I am fine!"

"And it sounds like we have that young man to thank."

"Yes."

"Promise me, you won't look at me differently when you find out what I've done."

"I promise."

"Yes, I killed in Germany. Tim Zhang."

A knot twisted in my stomach. I had proof my brother was a killer and worse, I had a sense of relief wash over me. What had happened to me that I could now feel relief in the death of another man, another human being. I hadn't started out this sick. Tears welled in my eyes.

"Don't cry, you will make it worse."

"I'm sorry…"

"Don't apologize. I did what I had to as my father's son and the deed is done. That man won't hurt you any longer."

I nodded and Vasily turned my chin up to face him.

"Feo and I have a plan. We are obligated to seek revenge on our sister's behalf. But I promise, if we can help it, I will not kill another German."

"Good."

"Papa will keep you safe while we are gone but in three months, we will have our opportunity and we must strike."

"I understand."

"Good. Milena, don't be afraid."

I hadn't heard the name Milena in too long. I hugged Vasily. The door thrust open without a knock and Feodor entered. He looked beat up. Bad.

"Disgusting," he sneered.

We pulled apart.

"Come here you."

Feodor hugged me, even tighter then Vasily. He stank like vodka already.

"Milena, welcome back home."

"Thank you."

He stared at me with a goofy smile on his face.

"I see the island turned you skinny. It is not good. Russian women must be fat. Thick!"

"Feo!" Vasily chided.

Feodor laughed.

"I brought vodka!"

We'd guessed by his smell, but neither of us was brave enough to tell him. Feodor sipped from his engraved flask and then passed it around to each of us to drink. We each chugged as much as we could before passing it around. Heat rushed to my face as the vodka slipped down my throat easily.

"You are much stronger at drinking vodka now, Milena," Feodor pointed out.

I smiled. He had Mace to thank for that and keeping up with the soldiers on the island. A wave of sadness for the men that had died washed over me. Perhaps Vasily and Feodor's obsession with revenge wasn't so wrong. It wouldn't only be revenge for me, but for Chester Chubb with his Bible-thumping, for Robbie and his gentle demeanor, or even for Bubba Ellis who had never been working for the Germans after all.

"What were you two talking about?"

"Berlin," Vasily told him.

Feo thumped me on the back.

"Don't worry, Milena. We will make those bastards pay. Pow! Pow!"

He mimed shooting them until Vasily saw the fallen expression on my face.

"Feo!"

"Sorry. She can't believe we'd take them out for drinks…" he grumbled.

"I promise. I will get a hold on him," Vasily said.

"What was your disagreement about anyway?" I asked the two of them.

They exchanged glances as if trying to agree on a story beforehand. Feodor pressed his hand to Vasily's chest and explained everything to me. They disagreed about a real estate acquisition Papa planned to make over in Paris. The disagreement had split them in two and Feodor had 'gone rogue' as he put it. He stirred up trouble in London to keep Vasily distracted. In the end, they'd resolved it all, like good brothers, over a bottle of vodka. They confessed that my disappearance was a catalyst for building better relations.

"Now Moscow is stronger than ever, and we control half the thugs in St. Petersburg. Feodor's little dalliance was a very good distraction that weakened our enemies and gave us time to advance our recruitment."

Half of what they said didn't make any sense to me, but I enjoyed my brothers finally trusting me enough to open up. Mace returned and Feodor glowered.

"Is this the bastard who is banging my sister?"

"FEO!"

He lunged at Mace with his fists clenched before Vasily

grabbed him and pulled him off. Mace looked embarrassed. Of course, he did not wish to fight my brothers, but if Feodor had hit him, he wouldn't have been able to hold back.

"Hi, the name's Feodor," he replied with an outstretched hand.

Mace took his hand reluctantly.

"What are you doing up here?"

"I spoke with your father, Aminata and I have something I'd like to ask."

"Do you need privacy?" Vasily asked.

Mace shook his head.

"No. It's better if you two are here."

Mace fumbled for something in his pocket and then got down on one knee.

"I didn't really plan this out that way I meant to, so I'm sorry, but as soon as I landed in America, I bought this…"

He pulled the small box out of his pocket and opened it, revealing a gold ring dripping in diamonds with a large, red stone in the center.

"Amy, will you please do me the honor of being my wife?"

My brothers' expressions had softened. Vasily gave me an encouraging nod. With shaking hands I accepted, and Mace slipped the ring onto my finger for me. The ring fit perfectly. The seven diamonds surrounding the ruby center were meant to symbolize the seven letters of my Sudanese name, Aminata. The single Ruby in the center reminded Mace of Russia. He'd been far more thoughtful than I could have imagined. Beneath his brutish, militaristic tendencies, there was a good man.

He kissed me with my brothers looking on for as long as they could stand, which was no longer than a few moments. Feodor cleared his throat and Mace apologized, pulling away with flushed cheeks.

"I expect you two have much to discuss," Vasily excused the two of them and they bustled out of the room, most likely to report on the status of my engagement to Papa. Once we were alone, Mace kissed me again, hard. He pressed me up against the wall with urgency and desire he'd done well to conceal in my brothers' presence.

When he pulled away, with reddened cheeks and his cock already rising in his trousers, I could hear his heartbeat syncopating with mine.

"Is it bad if I want to hold you and screw you up against this wall?"

"Why on earth would I say no to that?"

"This is why I love you…"

He hoisted me up and pressed me against the wall. I stroked my hand through his hair, which he hadn't cut since the island. My ring got caught in a few strands. He shook off the sharp tugs with a kiss.

"Guess you aren't used to being Mrs. Harwood yet…"

"Mrs. Harwood. It has a nice ring to it."

I squeezed my legs around his hips, drawing him closer to me. He pinned my arms above my head, holding them in place.

"You bad… bad… girl."

I kissed him back, no longer afraid to let him see my bad side.

"I can't believe I nearly lost you," he murmured, kissing my neck and running his fingers over the buttons of my shirt, undoing them one by one, and exposing my flesh to the suite's warmth. The warm lighting flickered in our room, where Papa had blended old Russian aesthetics with the recent modern updates.

"I nearly lost you. I ran off… If I hadn't run off we might have found Tim together."

"You ran off because I was being an asshole. I never want to make you question me, Aminata."

I knew he meant it, but it was too late, I'd already forgiven him. He'd been an asshole, but I'd been a princess, too spoiled and naive to realize the house of cards my perfect world was built on. Even now, I couldn't fully understand what kind of dangers my brothers and my father were up to. With Mace at my side, I would never be afraid again.

"The truth is, you saved my life on that island," Mace whispered, "I didn't think it was possible to love someone that much."

He knew just the right words to undo me. He tossed my blouse to the side and his hand cupped my breast as he ground his hips into me, thrusting me harder against the wall.

I was out of my pants before I realized it and with my legs spread around his torso, Mace's body burned like a furnace. He dropped to his knees, continuing to prop my weight up as he pressed me against the wall of our new bedroom. With my legs spread, he had easy access to my dripping pussy. From the moment his lips touched mine, I'd been dripping with anticipation and remained hungry for the soft massage of his lips and tongue against my sopping pussy lips.

He started with his fingers. Mace slid one finger between my lips with the gentle dexterity that you use to turn a page. He caressed each lip with his fingers and once his index finger was thoroughly coated in my juices, he brought it up to my engorged clit and began to make slow, precise circles. His gentle touch lit millions of my nerve endings ablaze with utter delight. Mace ensured that I moaned louder and louder with each stroke and once I was at the height of pleasure, moments away from spilling over into a pure, unfettered climax, he added his tongue into the mix.

With his tongue sliding between my pussy lips, I cried out one last time before climaxing. My wetness throbbed and a gush of juices rushed out of me, coating my thighs and forcing climax after climax through my body from the simple intensity of the release.

"Don't stop…" I murmured.

Mace never had any intentions of stopping until I was thoroughly exhausted from climaxing. He'd mentioned before that this was his favorite thing, getting down on his knees and controlling every aspect of my pleasure. He slipped one finger into my tightness as his tongue continued to massage my clit. He traced the alphabet along my folds, his tongue lapping at and teasing the most sensitive untouched areas of my pussy. As his tongue worked expertly, he buried two fingers deep inside me. I whimpered and cried out as he touched the deepest parts of my wetness, submitting both his tongue and hands to service my hunger for pleasure. I widened my legs, allowing him to drive deeper inside me as I came harder against his hands and lips. My juices coated his face and fingers as I climaxed repeatedly.

His fingers sank into my ass cheeks as he lifted me off the wall and moved me over to the bed.

"It's time we test this out…"

Spreading my sopping legs further apart, Mace kissed my inner thighs, tracing his tongue along my flesh as his lips traveled up to my mound and then past my mound over my stomach and breasts. His fingers followed his tongue, swirling around my nipples as I moaned and squealed from the anticipation. He pressed his torso between my thighs, his member bursting from his trousers with ferocious desire. I bucked my hips upward, enticing him to release his hardness and get on with it.

He grabbed my arms again, pinning them above my head.

"You're not in control here, princess," he growled.

Fuck. It was so hot when he took control like that. He was pure alpha in the bedroom — relentless, dominant and primal. The magnificent lovemaking we'd had in the woods hadn't been a product of the environment. Mace was wild every-where. He knew what I liked… what I wanted…

"I don't need to be in control with you," I murmured back.

He popped one of my nipples into his mouth and I moaned even louder, raking my hands through his hair, this time steering clear of getting my ring caught in his thick strands. He moved his lips back up to kiss me and he toyed with my lips until my wetness ached for him to fill me. He could sense my hunger for him mounting with each passing moment and his hand finally worked his buckle and zipper open as he released his cock.

"Mm," he murmured, "You're desperate for it, aren't you?"

"No…I'm not…"

"Don't lie to me, princess. I know you better than you realize."

He pressed the head of his cock against my entrance, holding it there and teasing me by rubbing the head between my lips, massaging my clit with the engorged bulbous head of his dick.

"Ohh, Mace…"

"See? I knew just how badly you wanted me. And now, I want you to beg."

"I will not…"

"Really?"

An impish smirk crossed his face as he massaged his cock between my lips, careful not to slide inside me. I whimpered and bucked my hips, not wanting to relent.

"Beg…"

"P-please…"

"That's right, princess. I want you to admit how much you want my cock."

"P-please… Give it to me. Give me that big white cock."

He chuckled mischievously.

"I love your filthy little mouth."

"Put that big white cock in my naughty little pussy," I replied.

"There it is… Good girl…"

He slipped his full length inside me with one swift motion. I cried out loud as his hardness touched the very depths of my wetness. His large cock stretched out every inch of my tightness and as he moved between my legs, unspeakable pleasure surged through every inch of me. Euphoria tightened at my core and then exploded forth with a climax unlike any I'd experienced before.

Mace kept my hands pinned above my head, holding me into the bed forcefully. He forced me to submit every bit of myself to him. I bucked and moaned as my hips eagerly accepted the assault by his large cock. He plunged into me deeper and the harder he pumped between my legs, the more I craved his complete dominance.

I'd been the woman too scared to give up control too many times before. With Mace, I could be free… He gripped my hips as he pushed his cock into my depths, panting and gasping for breath. When my eyes caught him, he grunted and gave me exactly what I wanted, his grunting, gruff thrusts as he used my body as a tool for his pleasure.

"Yes… Take me…" I moaned.

"I'm going to cum…" he grunted.

I spread my legs wider and he slowed his strokes to intense, rhythmic pumps between my legs. He released my hands from their prison and I clung to his back as he rocked his cock between my legs and I accepted every moment of intense pleasure that exploded from his slow, romantic strokes. He pushed the hair out of my face as he moved for those last few strokes between my legs and as he came, he kissed me, thrusting his tongue into my mouth as his cock erupted large rivers of cum between my legs.

We'd made a big mess and the mixture of our juices stained our thighs with stickiness. Mace pulled out of me, his cheeks red and hair sticking to his neck from sweat.

"I think it's time we get cleaned up."

"The showers in here are incredible."

And lucky us, we had yet to test them out. Wrapping white flannel sheets around our exposed bodies, we tiptoed through our private suite toward the bathroom. When we entered, automatic lights flashed on and a computerized voice announced, "Welcome. Please select the water temperature and bath products. We have three scents for you to choose from: lavender, eucalyptus or lemon."

"Holy shit, that's creepy."

"I'm sorry, I do not understand the request," the computer replied.

"Eucalyptus and… 78-degree water temperature."

The shower at the other end of the room turned on and Mace still looked like he'd seen a ghost.

"I can't believe you have a shower that talks."

"It's computerized! It's a smart home thing…"

"I think I like my homes stupid," Mace grumbled.

"Once you get in the water, you'll love it."

We walked to the back of the bathroom and I opened the

shower door. Three large shower heads rained down overhead.

"This is crazy…"

"Go on, get in."

I smacked Mace's butt, egging him into the shower. He flinched, but I saw a little smirk cross his face that told me he liked when I did those little things to show he was mine… My alpha… My SEAL.

"This reminds me of the Philippines," he said.

"I didn't know you went to the Philippines."

"Not for long. A two-day mission with the Army."

"Sounds top secret," I replied, wrapping my arms around his neck. He held my hips and we kissed in the shower. With the warmth and light water pressure, it was just like kissing in a light rainstorm. He ran his hands through my hair, soaking my curls with water.

"It is top secret," he replied.

"How will you being here affect things for you, Mace. With all this talk in America of Russian spies…"

He snorted.

"You don't believe that shit, do you?"

"There's proof of it."

"Captain Lorde knows where my loyalties lie."

"And my loyalty lies with you," I replied.

He kissed me again and ran his hands through my hair once

more. Talk of war, politics, or even diplomacy was enough to have him change the subject. When he was with me, Mace seemed to forget about his missions. I was all that mattered to him, and I liked that.

"I love your hair," he murmured.

I repeated the motion on him.

"I love yours."

"I don't want you to worry about politics," he murmured, "I'm here and that's what matters. And no matter what, I'm going to take care of you."

"Alright."

"I know your father is into a dangerous line of work, and I'll do my best to make sure it doesn't affect the two of us."

"Papa did give you permission to marry me."

"He did. And I'll make sure he doesn't regret that."

"What about me?"

"I know you won't regret it. Hell, I know about seven thousand ways to make you scream…"

He hoisted me up again and I squealed as he pressed me against the wall of the shower.

"In fact… I'd say I'm ready for round two…"

"I think that sounds like a wonderful idea, Officer Harwood."

"Officer? Now that's formal…"

"You like it though, don't you. Officer Harwood… Please

give me your cock… Please pound me against the shower wall until my pussy milks your cock for every drop of cum."

"My my my, Mrs. Harwood, what a filthy mouth you have…"

"Yes, sir. I guess you have no choice but to punish me."

THE END.

More Jamila Jasper Romance

Keep reading past this section to find out how to get Jamila Jasper books for FREE!

FULL CATALOG BY JAMILA JASPER:

http://jamilajasperromance.com/2018/05/07/complete-amazon-back-catalog-jamila-jasper-bwwm-romance-author/

NON-EXCLUSIVE INTERRACIAL ROMANCE TITLES:

http://jamilajasperromance.com/2018/01/12/nook-kobo-ibooks-google-play-bwwm-book-list-published-wide-interracial-romance/

JAMILA JASPER ROMANCE AUDIOBOOK COLLECTION:

http://jamilajasperromance.com/2018/01/12/bwwm-romance-

on-audio-book-jamila-jasper-interracial-romance-audio-
collection/

Patreon

EVEN MORE BONUS CONTENT FOR LESS THAN $2/MONTH:

I've just launched a new opportunity for you to get a "back-stage pass" to Jamila Jasper publishing by joining my Patreon!

For a small monthly fee, you get exclusive access to materials NOT available on my mailing list.

You'll receive:

Free short story audiobooks and audiobook samples when they're ready

#FirstDraftLeaks of Prologues and first chapters **weeks** before I hit publish

Notes from Jamila -- blog posts from my writing desk about my process so you can get to know the writer better

Click here to join: www.patreon.com/jamilajasper

Gold Subscribers, Platinum Subscribers, (and more) get more exclusive content: you can get characters named after you, a mention in my dedication and even participate in deciding KEY aspects of the plot.

Check out the tiered subscription plans starting at $1.49/month, less than your daily morning coffee!

Click here: www.patreon.com/jamilajasper

Afterword

Dear Reader,

Thank you so much for reading my book.

For making it all the way to the end of this book, I want to offer you a 🎁 **FREE gift**🎁 .

Sign up to my newsletter and receive **3 FREE BWWM romance novels**

- Keeping His Baby (Raven Ferrari)
- European Billionaire's Baby (Sugar Milan)
- Love Over Envy (Jamila Jasper)

You'll also receive: **FREE BWWM romance audiobook**:

- Making Me Crazy (BWWM Short Story) narrated by Jamila Jasper

If you LOVE reading romance and you want instant access to more FREE books, click the link below 👆

Click here to sign up: http://bit.ly/jamilajasper

Enjoy the freebies!

Jamila

If you LOVE reading romance and you want instant access to more FREE books, click the link below

Click here to sign up: http://bit.ly/jamilajasper

Social Media

Join me on social media! You'll find a reasonable number of daily posts, personal interaction & a welcoming community of interracial romance readers:

www.instagram.com/bwwmjamila

www.twitter.com/jamilajasper

www.facebook.com/bwwmjamila

jamilajasperromance@gmail.com

www.jamilajasperromance.com

Acknowledgments

Thank you to all my readers, new and old for your support with this new year. I look forward to making 2019 an INCREDIBLE year for interracial romance novels. I want to thank you all for joining along on the journey.